The Genius Prince's Guide to Raising a Nation out of Debt
(Hey, How About Treason?)

Toru Toba | Illustration Falmaro

CONTENTS

The Genius Prince's Guide to Raising a Nation Out of Debt (Hey, How About Treason?)

©Falmaro

✢ Ninym ✢

Wein

©Falmaro

Falanya

"Did he really... search for God?"

The siblings were discussing the history of a particular civilization. The ancient Flahm people, to be exact.

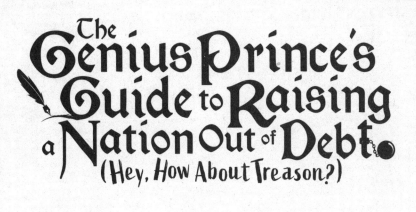

The Genius Prince's Guide to Raising a Nation Out of Debt
(Hey, How About Treason?)

9

Toru Toba

Illustration **Falmaro**

YEN ON

New York

The Genius Prince's Guide to Raising a Nation Out of Debt (Hey, How About Treason?)

9

Toru Toba

Translation by Jessica Lange
Cover art by Falmaro

TENSAI OUJI NO AKAJI KOKKA SAISEI-JYUTSU ~ SOUDA, BAIKOKU SHIYOU ~ volume 9
Copyright © 2021 Toru Toba
Illustrations copyright © 2021 Falmaro
All rights reserved.
Original Japanese edition published in 2021 by SB Creative Corp.

This English edition is published by arrangement with SB Creative Corp., Tokyo in care of Tuttle-Mori Agency, Inc., Tokyo.

English translation © 2022 by Yen Press, LLC

Yen On
150 West 30th Street, 19th Floor
New York, NY 10001

Visit us at yenpress.com
facebook.com/yenpress
twitter.com/yenpress
yenpress.tumblr.com
instagram.com/yenpress

First Yen On Edition: May 2022

Yen On is an imprint of Yen Press, LLC.
The Yen On name and logo are trademarks of Yen Press, LLC.

The publisher is not responsible for websites (or their content) that are not owned by the publisher.

Library of Congress Cataloging-in-Publication Data
Names: Toba, Toru, author. | Falmaro, illustrator. | Lange, Jessica (Translator), translator.
Title: The genius prince's guide to raising a nation out of debt (hey, how about treason?) / Toru Toba ; illustration by Falmaro ; translation by Jessica Lange.
Other titles: Tensai ouji no akaji kokka saisei-jyutsu, souda, baikoku shiyou. English
Description: First Yen On edition. | New York, NY : Yen On, 2019–
Identifiers: LCCN 2019017156| ISBN 9781975385194 (v. 1 : pbk.) | ISBN9781975385170 (v. 2 : pbk.) |
    ISBN 9781975309985 (v. 3 : pbk.) | ISBN 9781975310004 (v. 4 : pbk.) | ISBN 9781975313708 (v. 5 : pbk.) |
    ISBN 9781975319830 (v. 6 : pbk.) | ISBN 9781975321604 (v. 7 : pbk.) | ISBN 9781975335878 (v. 8 : pbk.) |
    ISBN 9781975339111 (v. 9 : pbk)
Subjects: LCSH: Princes—Fiction.
Classification: LCC PL876.O25 T4613 2019 | DDC 895.6/36—dc23
LC record available at https://lccn.loc.gov/2019017156

ISBNs: 978-1-9753-3911-1 (paperback)
        978-1-9753-3912-8 (ebook)

10 9 8 7 6 5 4 3 2 1

LSC-C

Printed in the United States of America

The Genius Prince's Guide to Raising a Nation Out of Debt

(Hey, How About Treason?)

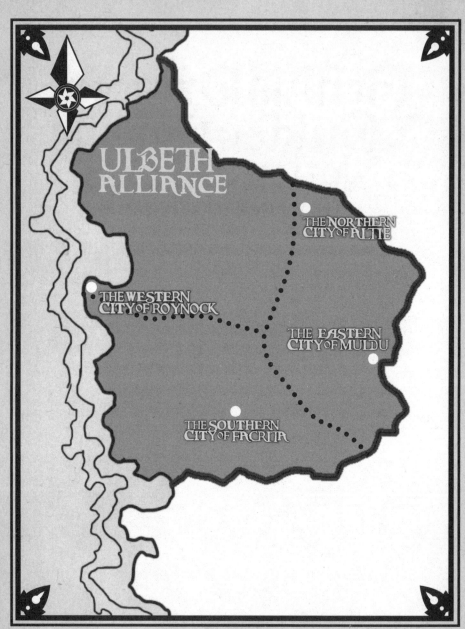

ULBETH ALLIANCE

THE NORTHERN CITY OF ALTIE

THE WESTERN CITY OF ROYNOCK

THE EASTERN CITY OF MULDU

THE SOUTHERN CITY OF FACRITA

©Falmaro

WEIN

Prince regent of the continent's northern-most country, the Kingdom of Natra. A born genius who rescued his nation from many a disaster. Renowned as a benevo-lent leader, but is actually a self-indulgent slacker with everything except personality and looks.

 FALANYA

Wein's little sister and the crown princess of Natra. Idolizes her brother and studies tirelessly in hopes of helping him. Made her negotiation debut during the Gathering of the Chosen in the old capital of Lushan. Sir-gis, former prime minister of the Delunio Kingdom, is her trusted retainer.

NANAKI
Falanya's guard. A Flahm like Ninym. While not very expressive, he cares deeply for Falanya.

LEJOUTTE
A young woman whose advanced agri-cultural methods helped Facrita develop rapidly. Works hard to lead her city as its representative.

 NINYM

Wein's childhood friend and his Heart. Serves as his aide in the public and private sphere. Wishes Wein wouldn't be so reckless. Part of the Flahm, a group that's persecuted in the West.

 AGATA

Representative of Muldu, one of the four cities in the Ulbeth Alliance. He's also their international spokesman and a Holy Elite. Asks Wein to help him unite the crumbling union.

KAMIL
Agata's right-hand man. He knows Ninym is a Flahm but doesn't mind.

OLEOM
A young man who represents Roynock, a city known for its rich maritime trade. He's concerned with the shifting balance of power in the Ulbeth Alliance.

©Falmaro

It began long, long ago.

One driven man set out on a journey. His oppressed and enslaved people, stripped of their pride and cultural heritage, found no salvation in this life or the next. Cries for rescue went unheard, a master's whip and scorn their only reward.

"You slaves have no god. Your only fate is to be mocked, persecuted, and consumed."

Most of his brethren suffered this derision in silence. After all, no words could save them. Despite endless trials and tribulations, emancipation never arrived. It was enough to leave one wondering if the gods despised them.

He was different, however.

"Our divine savior is somewhere on this vast continent. They just haven't heard us yet."

That was his conviction.

"However long it takes, I'll find a god to deliver the Flahm."

With that, he departed on a holy quest. His name is long forgotten. Posterity only knows this traveler with the fiery red hair and bright crimson eyes as the "Founder."

"—And that man was the father of the Flahm Kingdom."

A young man sat by a roaring fireplace, a book in one hand. It was Wein Salema Arbalest, the crown prince of the Natra Kingdom. Together with the gentle snow outside the window, the hearth created a cozy atmosphere.

"Did he really…search for God?" asked the youthful girl with him by the fire. Her name was Falanya Elk Arbalest, and she was Wein's younger sister and Natra's crown princess.

The siblings were discussing the history of a particular civilization. The ancient Flahm people, to be exact.

"Yes, at least according to our records here in Natra. Of course, we're talking about an event from centuries ago. It's hard to know what someone was thinking back then."

Still, we can't discount written history, Wein implied wordlessly.

"So did the Founder succeed?" Falanya asked, but her brother continued without answering.

"The Founder chased every holy lead across the continent. Apparently, he even marched into forbidden sanctums and exposed the gods despite local protest. His actions made him the target of attacks by several different religious groups."

"He must have been truly desperate."

The Founder ignored his own peril in pursuit of God and left no stone, figurative or literal, unturned. All so he could bring meager peace to his suffering friends, comrades, and loved ones.

"However, his wish never came true."

"What?" Falanya questioned, her eyes large.

"Ancient societies believed in far more numerous gods and spirits than those of the modern day. That spectrum ranged from nature worship in primitive animism to polytheistic systems ruled by a central deity. Among these, the Founder likely converted to the oldest religion—atheism."

The Founder spent long years searching every corner of the continent and risking his own life—yet he never found a divine protector for the Flahm.

After demystifying the gods he'd yearned for, the forlorn Founder must have concluded the continent was home only to false idols.

"He didn't find God…but built the Flahm Kingdom anyway?"

"That's right. At first, the Founder was heartbroken, but he quickly hatched a diabolical plan: If God didn't exist, he would invent one to suit the Flahm." Wein paused to grin. "And thus, the continent's first monotheism was born."

Sirgis, former prime minister of the Delunio Kingdom and current vassal to Natra's crown princess Falanya, entered the room and felt a slight wave of regret wash over him. He'd come looking for his master but found someone he'd give anything to avoid.

"Oh? May I help you, Sir Sirgis?"

Ninym Ralei, the one who posed the question, tilted her head. She was Crown Prince Wein's aide and, as evidenced by her white hair and red eyes, a Flahm.

"…Might I ask where Princess Falanya is?" Sirgis asked, his expression sour.

"She's in that room," Ninym readily answered, pointing to a door nearby. "However, Her Highness and Prince Wein are in the middle of a discussion."

"I see… In that case, I shall return later."

Sirgis turned to leave, but Ninym called out behind him.

"It's almost time for Prince Wein to return to his government affairs. Would you like to wait here for a while?"

It wasn't an odd proposal, but Sirgis groaned quietly.

"...I had intended to show you courtesy."

"There's no need. After all, we both serve Natra's royal family."

"You feel no reservation toward me?"

"If anything, shouldn't it be the other way around? After all, you are a devout follower of Levetia."

"..."

The Teachings of Levetia was the biggest religion in the West. Its doctrine persecuted the Flahm, so Natra's tolerance shocked Western visitors.

"...Yes, I used to accept the Teachings of Levetia blindly. However, that is all in the past," Sirgis responded, pulling up a chair. "You're right, Lady Ninym. As fellow vassals, we must be open with one another."

Ninym smiled faintly as Sirgis looked away in irritation. He mulled over how to best answer this composed girl over a decade his junior.

"By the way, why aren't you with Their Highnesses?" he blurted out.

It was a silly question, but Sirgis was curious all the same. Ninym accompanied Wein everywhere as his guard, so she'd typically be in the room with him instead of waiting outside the door. Why the sudden change?

"They're discussing Flahm history," explained the young woman. "Some topics would be difficult if I were present."

"...Flahm history, you say?"

"I can go into detail if you're interested."

"I shall pass," Sirgis replied curtly. Then he recalled something that had long weighed on his mind. "Well, this isn't about the Flahm precisely, but there's something I've been meaning to ask... Why does the Natran royal family hold your people in such esteem?"

Natra's acceptance of the Flahm was odd by Western standards, but the long line of Flahm aides to the royal family was stranger still. Keeping traditions like those was unfathomable in the West, and even those in the East rarely limited their assistants to a single clan.

"In short, it began with a promise made a century ago."

"A promise?"

"A group of persecuted Flahm led by a man named Ralei fled to Natra and demonstrated their knowledge and skills to the royal family in exchange for protection. The king was so moved that he made Ralei his aide."

"What an open-minded ruler to keep the Flahm so close despite the cost."

"I've heard that Natra saw fewer visitors after Levetia announced the Circulous Law. The traditional pilgrimage used Natra as a gateway across the continent, but new regulations stated that a circuit around the West was enough. In other words, appointing the Flahm was partly done for revenge."

"I see. Yes, that sounds plausible," Sirgis said with a faint, wry smile.

Still, a relationship built on such motives was doomed to fail.

"As you've noticed, the key part came afterward. Ralei dedicated his life to the king, who respected both Ralei and the Flahm. The two men shared a deep trust to their final days. The Flahm volunteered their skills to the royal family, and the royal family generously provided refuge."

It was like a promise between children. Those involved were already on thin ice, so a multigenerational oath was mere fantasy. Everyone must have believed the alliance would crumble once its founders were gone—even the king and Ralei.

However, their vow lasted an entire century and became an established custom.

"Countless royals and Flahm have continued to honor this pact. It was no small feat, but we Flahm aides are now a natural part of Natran society."

"...I suppose there's an odd chapter in every nation's history," Sirgis remarked with a nod of understanding. "Are only the most talented Flahm chosen to serve the royal family?"

"For the most part, but there are some exceptions. Princess Falanya chose Nanaki personally. In my case—"

Just then, Wein's head popped out from the room next door.

"Sorry 'bout the wait, Ninym. Oh, Sirgis. You're here, too?"

Both Ninym and Sirgis bowed respectfully.

"Have you finished your discussion?" Ninym inquired.

"Yeah, but it took forever. Ah! Watch it!"

A melancholy Falanya suddenly appeared behind Wein. When the princess saw Ninym, she pushed past him and ran to squeeze the older girl.

"Wh-whatever is the matter, Princess Falanya?" Ninym asked, startled by her unexpected behavior.

Falanya lifted her head from Ninym's shoulder. "...I don't care what others did in the past."

Sirgis didn't grasp the meaning, but a kind smile spread across Ninym's face.

"Your Highness, those words alone ease the hearts of all Flahm."

Although different races, the pair appeared like sisters as Ninym accepted Falanya's embrace and stroked her hair. Their shared history wove a tangible harmony between them.

"Did you need me, Sirgis?" Wein said, breaking Sirgis's contemplation.

"No, I wish to confirm a few matters with Princess Falanya about an upcoming meeting."

"Gotcha." Wein nodded. "Give her a minute, though. She's still processing her feelings."

"Yes, understood."

I'm sure there are shocking aspects of Flahm history, Sirgis thought. If one delved into the continent's history, they would find several grisly truths. Falanya was a princess, but also a child. No one could blame her for being upset.

That's right... She's still a child.

Since Sirgis became Falanya's vassal, he had come to understand that she was a capable royal. Her passion and ambition were evident, and she had an equal measure of intelligence. Falanya took advice yet refused to be spoon-fed.

Given a decade to mature, the frail, inexperienced princess would be an excellent politician.

However, there was one significant caveat.

Even the gifted Falanya was no match for her older brother, Wein. A survey of one hundred people would be unanimously in favor of the elder sibling.

This won't be easy.

Sirgis would install Princess Falanya on Natra's throne. That was his goal as an ex–prime minister (courtesy of Wein) and as Falanya's vassal.

I can't rush things. However, there's no telling when the current king will abdicate to the prince. I'll need both stealth and haste...

Did Wein realize there was a turncoat in his midst? Most certainly. He was a genius prince, after all. Still, the young royal said nothing. There was no telling if that was due to carelessness or because he had other plans. Sirgis felt uneasy, but his objective remained the same. He would use every opportunity to support Falanya.

"...Incidentally, I hear you'll be traveling abroad soon, Prince."

"Yeah, to the Ulbeth Alliance. Know anything about it?"

"I've visited the region on numerous occasions. It is a...peculiar nation."

"Oh? How so?"

"Both Natra and Delunio have unique cultures and traditions, but the well-established Ulbeth Alliance is distinct to an abnormal degree," Sirgis replied.

"Hmm...I've heard they've been around awhile. Culture and tradition, huh?"

Wein tried to conjure a mental picture of the unfamiliar country and groaned quietly.

Falanya, having regained her composure, called to him. "Wein, you're going to Ulbeth on business, right?"

"Yeah. Natra's trade with Patura took a major hit during the last Gathering of the Chosen, so I need to hurry and do damage control. I'm sure Ulbeth's representative, the Holy Elite named Agata, won't stop there, though. Negotiations should be interesting."

Falanya sheepishly eyed the prince. "Please be careful, Wein. The previous Gathering of the Chosen looked safe at the beginning. Even if you expect a regular meeting, there's no telling what might happen."

The chaos from last autumn's Gathering of the Chosen still cast a shadow over Falanya's heart.

"No worries, Falanya. Stuff like that is one in a million," Wein assured her with an amused grin. He ruffled his sister's hair. "Still, I'll need you to watch the homestead while I'm gone. Sirgis, help her out, okay?"

"You can count on me, Wein!"

"Yes. Leave everything to us."

Falanya was bursting with enthusiasm, while Sirgis merely gave a formal bow. The genius prince smiled and nodded in satisfaction.

Several days later, a delegation led by Wein departed for the Ulbeth Alliance. Falanya, who saw them off, would later ask herself the following:

"I wonder if everything that happened in the Ulbeth Alliance that winter hinted at the future awaiting my brother and the others."

In the future, this period came to be known as the "Great War of Kings."

The Ulbeth Alliance was a nation consisting of four city-states that had fought over the hegemony of the coast of the West prior to unification. The quartet constantly waffled between allies and enemies, and battle raged. However, as trade and communication extended beyond the Far West, leaders worried about growing foreign pressure.

"Won't other nations overtake us if we keep fighting like this?"

"Still, it'll be tough to join forces now."

"No…it might be easier than we think."

Around the same time, solidarity among the cities' people was curiously on the rise. Foreign culture was strange and incomprehensible, but the citizens of all four city-states shared regional commonalities. Because of this, they sympathized more with familiar rivals than unknown outsiders. Of course, some believed their shared history of bloodshed meant cooperation was out of the question. A neighboring conqueror was better than a foreign one, though.

As public sentiment and politics mixed, the four cities came together to form a kind of allied nation rarely seen on the continent.

"A coalition of city-states is quite ambitious." Ninym skimmed over documents inside a carriage headed for the Ulbeth Alliance. "Holy Elite Agata is their international spokesman, but the government is run by city representatives who share equal authority… It's like having several kings in one country, yet they make it work." She glanced at the man in front of her. "Wouldn't you agree, Wein?"

Her master was presently staring out the window.

"Yeah. A parliamentary system isn't uncommon, but not many city-states push the limits of an alliance and agree to equal representation." Judging by his tone, Wein was impressed with Ulbeth. "Trailblazing means fewer examples to work from, so it's a real challenge. Neighboring countries aren't a great reference when your own method breaks the mold. Most are monarchies, so Natra stole a page right out of the handbook."

A government was a nation's template, and it was easier to copycat when everyone around you had similar standards. A country could last one hundred years or more, far beyond the human lifetime. Therefore, creating laws and systems that were unconventional or only benefited you were impractical. It was best to be mindful of neighboring powers.

As Wein stated, the Ulbeth Alliance's unique approach came with difficulties. The union was undoubtedly fumbling, but their tenacious politicians kept things moving.

"You seem quite dazzled for someone who represents a monarchy."

"No one political system is 'correct.' What matters is how people benefit from it. Who cares if the government is 'on your side' if everyone starves to death? Do whatever works."

"…Never repeat that in public. It'll be terrible PR."

"Oh yeah?" Wein replied casually.

Ninym sighed. She was the one who had raised the subject, but Wein's unorthodox comments kept her on her toes.

"Anyway, the Ulbeth Alliance seemingly has its own plans."

"…You mean the new unification Agata mentioned?"

Wein was visiting Ulbeth to discuss a deal that Agata, an Alliance representative and Holy Elite, had proposed.

"I plan to take advantage of the Alliance's demise to unify the cities into one nation. Prince Wein, I am here to ask for your aid—"

The Gathering of the Chosen had been held the previous fall in the old capital of Lushan. Wein had just put an end to a tangled conspiracy and was about to head home when Agata approached him. Coincidentally, Natra's trade had recently suffered a harsh blow. Wein agreed to Agata's deal under the condition that Natra and Ulbeth become business partners.

"I wonder what Agata is planning."

"Good question. He's already a Holy Elite, and I didn't get a power-hungry vibe from him… Well, we'll know soon enough. Look, there it is." Wein pointed to the window. Ninym looked out beside him, and her eyes widened.

"That's…"

"I hear it's their national symbol. The four cities built the wall when the Alliance first came together. It's called the 'Rampart of Unity.'"

A single, endless wall stretched across the plain. The structure surrounded all four city-states. It was a worthy symbol of the Alliance, but the amount of labor it must have demanded was unfathomable.

Even so…

Parts of the edifice were cracked and crumbling. Perhaps long years of wind and rain had taken their toll.

Ninym felt like it reflected the present state of the Ulbeth Alliance.

The quartet of cities that made up the Ulbeth Alliance were divided into cardinal directions. Their shared closeness to the edge of the Western continent fostered a common culture between them, but even slight geographic differences gave each settlement a distinct character.

For example, the Great Blue Skies of Roynock, the westernmost of the four cities, enjoyed prosperous maritime trade because it was on the coast. The northern city, the Black Iron of Altie, was named for its many smiths. The southern settlement was blessed with abundant crops and thus was known as the Grand Red Harvest of Facrita.

Finally, the White Willow of Muldu to the east was notable for sitting directly across from western Roynock. In other words, Muldu was the continent's inland entrance to the western shores. It was the first town beyond the Rampart of Unity, and frequent contact with foreign visitors and cultures made this city's representative an ideal candidate for speaking on the Ulbeth Alliance's behalf.

And that person was Agata Willow.

"...It's almost time," Agata murmured as he gazed at the town outside his window.

"Did you say something, Master Agata?" his assistant asked. The man's head was cocked to one side.

"Why, I was just thinking everything will soon be blanketed in white."

"Indeed. Snow piles up quickly, thanks to the early sunset."

"The winter air brings many aches to these old bones. I already long for spring."

Judging by the overcast clouds, the precipitation could begin at any moment. There was a world of difference between the room temperature and the chill beyond the walls.

"Our upcoming events must proceed smoothly if we wish to welcome spring, correct?"

"Hmph, indeed. I trust preparations for the Signing Ceremony are going well?"

The aide nodded. "Everything is almost ready."

"Good. The event cannot afford any missteps."

"I've also just received word that Prince Wein's delegation has passed the Rampart of Unity."

"Then they are in Muldu and should be arriving shortly. Kamil, prepare to greet them."

"Yes, sir."

The aide bowed respectfully, and Agata gave him a sidelong glance before returning his attention to the window.

Yes, it's almost time. Prince Wein's arrival will signal the demise of the Ulbeth Alliance...

With dark, secret resolve, Agata eagerly awaited his visitors.

"Hey, those handicrafts are neat."

"I agree. That stall over there is also lined with masks. Maybe they're talismans of some kind?"

"Pretty creepy if you ask me... There's no guessing what culture invented those."

Shortly after passing the Rampart of Unity, Wein's delegation arrived in the eastern city of Muldu. Both the prince and Ninym offered their opinions on the local decoration as they rode by in the carriage.

"Regardless, the gateway to the Alliance is as lively as you'd expect."

As Wein said, a bustling crowd was milling around Muldu's entrance. Citizens, merchants, pilgrims, and more came together to paint a prosperous image.

"That's also why the carriage is now stuck in traffic."

"We can get a good look at the town, so it all works out."

"Fair enough. I've noticed most of the clothes and buildings are white. Is it a symbolic color?"

Wein nodded.

The White Willow of Muldu. True to its moniker, the city was enveloped in an alabaster shade. A heavy snowstorm would erase all other colors.

"The Ulbeth Alliance's unique cultures and customs are apparent from the second you set foot on its lands," Wein stated with evident interest. "Still, it doesn't feel *that* bizarre."

"I agree. Most of the architecture is typical of the West."

The Ulbeth Alliance had been born from fear of foreign pressure, and Sirgis said the nation was peculiar.

Thus, Wein and Ninym had mentally prepared for the view of a lifetime. Yet it seemed their anticipation was for naught.

"Well, a boring trip is fine by me."

"Wein, you spark trouble with the tiniest ember."

"You seem confused, so let me clarify. I am a man of *peace*."

"Such claims don't match your track record."

"That's because, while I love peace, it doesn't necessarily reciprocate."

"Keep talking like that, and you'll be trapped in a one-sided relationship."

Wein laughed. "You're probably right."

Ninym sighed and peered out the window again. Then she realized something abruptly. "...Wein," she said, her eyes narrowing.

"Yeah, I know," the prince replied, nodding slightly. "The mood changes the closer we get to the center of town."

The carriage had crossed the business district while they were talking and was approaching the administrative sector at the heart of Muldu.

Agata's mansion was ahead, so they were on the right path. However, unlike the cheery passersby in the business district, the atmosphere here was weighty and biting.

"Are outsiders only welcome as far as the main road?" Ninym inquired, her vigilance rising.

The eyes of those staring at the foreign delegation's carriage weren't just curious. They also brimmed with gloomy mistrust and doubt.

Wein flashed Ninym an arrogant smile. "Using foreigners instead of banning 'em outright, huh? Nice. The Ulbeth Alliance is savvier than I thought."

"Don't forget you said you wanted a boring trip."

"Oh, I definitely do. But still—"

The carriage stopped in front of a white mansion with a willow emblem engraved into the wall. This was the home of Agata, the East Representative of the Ulbeth Empire.

"We should assume there's already a fire burning beneath us."

Wein and Ninym alighted from the carriage together. A strapping young man greeted them.

"I've been expecting you, Prince Wein."

He was slightly older than Wein, and his black outfit popped against the white façade of the manor. With a respectful bow, he said, "My name is Kamil. I serve Master Agata. Please, right this way. I shall bring you to him."

Kamil ushered Wein inside, with Ninym and the delegation

guards in tow. The interior was clean and organized—likely a reflection of Agata himself. The artwork on display clearly shared the same roots as the street handicrafts, but a single glance made it apparent these were far more refined.

"Is this Sir Agata's collection?"

"Yes. More specifically, it has been curated by Master Agata and previous generations of the Willow family."

"I see. I'm not too familiar with artwork from this region, but the Willow family has an eye for beauty."

"Your intuition is quite sharp. Indeed, each is a priceless hand-picked piece. That tapestry was dyed with a technique that has since been lost."

Wein gathered intel as he chatted with Kamil.

Meanwhile, the prince's guards remained understandably cautious. After all, this was the stronghold of a foreign leader.

Carelessness was impermissible. Ninym, who was hiding in the back, felt the same way.

I should confirm the number of the guards and their positions. We also need an escape plan.

After recounting their endless troubles since Wein's rise to the position of regent, Ninym felt one could never be too wary. As the prince had said, there was a good chance the fire had already been lit.

Agata is our first option...but would Kamil also make a decent hostage?

It was a disturbing thought to entertain, but Ninym wanted multiple safeguards, just in case. Kamil was a refined man who had been entrusted with Wein's arrival. There was no doubt Agata valued him. However...

Just then, Kamil turned around.

Agh!

Ninym quickly ducked her head and looked away. She must have been staring too much. Luckily, Kamil said nothing and returned to his conversation with Wein. Ninym relaxed a bit but lightly fidgeted with a lock of her hair.

He didn't notice…right?

Ninym had dyed it black to mask her Flahm identity, but there was no concealing her red eyes. She could be exposed if she wasn't careful, and Ninym wanted to avoid unnecessary trouble.

Especially since, from what we've seen, Ulbeth isn't too fond of foreigners.

Keeping a close eye on her surroundings was paramount. Ninym's thoughts were interrupted when the party arrived at a large door.

"Master Agata, I've brought Prince Wein."

"Enter."

Kamil opened the door to a reception room, where an older man sat patiently. It was Agata Willow, a Holy Elite and representative of the White Willow of Muldu.

"It's been a while, Prince Wein."

"I'm glad to see you looking well, Sir Agata."

Agata was old enough to be Wein's grandfather. Nonetheless, both wore the same kind of smile.

They both look like a fighter paired against a worthy opponent, Ninym mused.

"Did the snow trouble you on the way here?"

"No, we were fortunate enough to arrive before it piled up. I can't say what the journey home will be like, however."

Discussion between the representatives of the Natra Kingdom and Ulbeth Alliance began amicably.

"If it proves bothersome, you can cross the sea to Soljest."

"I'm afraid I don't do well on boats. I'm hoping we have a mild winter."

Both men were high-ranking, but because of the age gap, the elder Agata maintained a composed air, and Wein showed due respect.

It's all an act, though.

All present in the room, Ninym included, sensed this. Buried beneath this congenial atmosphere were two hidden, snarling beasts.

"Ho-ho. So even Prince Wein has a weakness? After your impressive display at the last Gathering of the Chosen, I find that hard to believe."

"Was it so astounding? I simply nudged matters in the direction they were already headed."

"That little push has left a great impact on numerous countries," Agata responded with a slight grin. "The Kingdom of Valencia criticized Levetia for Prince Tigris's death during the Gathering of the Chosen, and their relationship is at a historic low. Steel of the Vanhelio Kingdom received severe internal backlash for mobilizing an army almost entirely on his own. And just as the Falcasso Kingdom predicted a famine, Eastern Levetia distributed free food. I hear that support for their royal family is wavering."

Naturally, these developments were creating problems for Wein as well. A mess like the Gathering of the Chosen wasn't easily cleaned up.

"I hear the threat of starvation looms over not just Falcasso but other Western nations as well. Fortunately, Natra has nothing to worry about. But goodness, this winter will be hard on everyone."

Wein gave a brazen smile. "Hopefully, leaders will be able to handle any foreign interlopers that might crop up during this difficult period."

"…"

Agata suddenly raised one hand. His guards and Kamil departed the room at once.

Ninym and the Natran guards turned to Wein for instruction. He gave a curt nod, prompting them to leave as well.

Now Wein and Agata were the only ones left.

"Well then, shall we get started?" Agata said solemnly.

After Ninym and the guards had exited, Kamil led them to an antechamber for servants. Of course, one of Wein's guards stood in front of the reception door as a precaution. Ninym would have done the job herself but prioritized blending in.

I hope the meeting goes well…

What deal could those two be making? Nothing good, no doubt. Still, she hoped it would at least end amicably.

As her mind raced with speculation, a voice called out to her.

"Might I ask your name?"

It was Kamil.

For a second, Ninym glanced around the room to check if he was speaking to another. When she saw him look straight at her, she hesitantly replied, "…It's Ninym. Ninym Ralei."

Kamil gave a small nod. "Ah, I thought so."

"Thought what?"

"I heard rumors that Prince Wein is accompanied by a skilled aide named Ninym."

It was foolishly optimistic to assume Kamil knew only her name by this point. Even cursory research would reveal the Natran royal family kept Flahm retainers.

"...With all due respect, you should keep your distance from me."

The uninformed might consider such a rebuke impolite. Kamil smiled, however.

"I believe a person's true worth is determined not by birth but by life choices."

"That is a fine sentiment. However, I doubt everyone will agree with your ideology."

"Chasing approval will only lead to a dry fountain."

"Yet, as one suffering from thirst, they have my sympathy."

"In that case, as one who is well nourished, I choose to share my bounty."

"......"

Ninym sighed. This gentle-looking but ridiculously stubborn man wasn't going to back down. Kamil's good intentions were problematic. She could have shaken him off had he been hostile. This was a more vexing predicament.

"I shall address you as 'Sir Kamil.'"

Ninym extended a hand in resignation. The young man happily took it.

"Just 'Kamil' is fine."

"I have no title, so please forgive me for adhering to formality."

"In that case, I will call you 'Lady Ninym.' As fellow aides, there is something I thought we'd best discuss."

"...Very well."

Ninym had planned to stay inconspicuous, and this was an unexpected twist. Regardless, the situation was out of her hands

now. Thinking the conversation might prove informative, Ninym elected to indulge Kamil until Wein's return.

"Do you know about Ulbeth's upcoming Signing Ceremony?"

Wein gave a small nod. "I heard it's a conference held once every ten years. The city representatives discuss different topics, including the pros and cons of the Alliance itself."

"Correct. During the Signing Ceremony, each city can also choose to withdraw. Equality is a founding principle of our nation."

"But no one actually goes through with it, right?" Wein questioned.

"From what I understand, the four cities' industries and economies are tightly interwoven. If one secedes, it'll either go bankrupt or be invaded by the other three."

Because of this, the Signing Ceremony had long since become an opportunity for each city to show off. Wein had been told that most citizens saw it as the party of the decade rather than a meaningful event that decided their futures.

"You're right," Agata agreed. "However, times have changed recently."

"Oh…?"

The Holy Elite grew visibly uneasy, and Wein's eyes sparkled with interest.

"Prince, what do you think is needed to maintain a union?"

"Equality," Wein replied without a second thought. "Alliances can form when both sides share a common enemy, but maintaining that bond is a different story. When there's a power gap, the strain grows over time."

Agata nodded gravely. "That is the issue the Ulbeth Alliance currently faces."

"What do you mean?"

"The eastern city of Muldu has ever been a gateway to the rest of the country. Whether incoming or outgoing, we handled almost everything. This gave Muldu value despite having no defined industry. However, in the past several decades, Roynock has increased their flow of goods and people thanks to improved shipbuilding techniques and established sea routes," Agata explained. "The fertile lands of Facrita to the south are similar. Because of recent agricultural advancements, their harvests have grown tenfold. Moreover, they largely export through Roynock."

"I see," Wein answered in understanding.

The south could harvest more. The west could export more. The two cities were undoubtedly growing close. Moreover, since time immemorial, the wealthiest regions have always made the best trade partners. And that growing profit was enough to shift the Alliance's power dynamics.

"Is it safe to say that Roynock and Facrita plan to unite as a separate entity, then?"

"That's likely their end game, but it can't happen all at once. Roynock and Facrita will work in stages by, for example, driving me out and appointing their own yes-man as the East Representative."

"So even one of your position isn't set for life?"

"Correct. Although representatives hold great power, we must have the support of various leaders. Losing that endorsement means forfeiting our position. Muldu representatives even inherit the title of Holy Elite."

Agata was a Holy Elite because he was the public face of the

Ulbeth Alliance. He'd have to give up both roles to his successor if he ceased acting as East Representative.

"…If I were leading Muldu, I'd try to win over Altie."

The eastern city desperately wanted to interrupt Facrita and Roynock's love affair. However, since that wasn't in the cards, they would have to devise a Plan B. This meant teaming up with the northern city to balance out the Alliance.

Agata quickly shot down Wein's proposal, though.

"That's impossible. Altie has a poor relationship with Muldu… No, with the entire Ulbeth Alliance."

"Really? Why?"

"Twenty years ago, the North Representative colluded with another nation. He and his entire family were executed. The other three cities used this opportunity to make representative succession hereditary. This meant that Altie was unable to choose anyone new since their last representative's bloodline had run dry."

"Well…that's certainly something."

A body of delegates ran the Ulbeth Alliance. It was also stipulated that no city could participate in the conference without one.

"So basically, the other three cities oppressed the northern one for their benefit."

Altie citizens could only watch as disadvantages were heaped upon them because they lacked the necessary official. It was unsurprising that they grew resentful and yearned to secede.

"The northern city will be thoroughly crushed if they withdraw, so they've had no recourse but to bottle up their discontent. Ha-ha. They must really hate your guts. Still, you've only got yourself to blame," Wein observed casually.

"If you'll let me clarify—"

"What? Are you going to say you didn't expect the south and the west to take the lead or something? You're better than that, Agata."

"...Yes, I misspoke. Disregard my comment."

Wein gave a slight shrug. "Anyway," he continued, "I get what's happening now. The west and the south took control, Altie is furious, and you're being driven into a corner. Forget foreign threats. The internal pressure alone is lethal."

"That's why I've invited you here, Prince Wein."

Agata's tone was noticeably mild. "I will use this as a golden opportunity to unite Ulbeth under Muldu. The first step is to create a rift between the west and the south. To do that, I'd like to borrow your rare intellect."

Agata bowed to the prince, who was less than half his age. Although there were no witnesses, national leaders seldom went to such lengths. Most recipients would feel more apologetic than awestruck.

Wein, of course, wasn't moved by this display.

"...Driving a wedge between the south and the west makes sense. They're problematic as a team, but Roynock and Facrita might turn on each other if both expect their own city to lead the new union. That discord could give you an opening. Still, I'm an outsider. What can I do?"

Wein was a foreign visitor in every aspect. He'd brought more than enough personnel, supplies, and money for one person, but he couldn't take on an entire country.

"The West Representative will be hosting a banquet soon, and I expect the South Representative will attend as well. I've added your name to the guest list, so meet them and get a sense of their characters."

"And after that?"

"I'll share my plan once you return. I think you'll appreciate it."

"…"

Wein fell silent for a moment and stared at Agata. His fiery gaze seemed to pierce the Holy Elite straight through. Agata felt as if his stomach were being wrenched open. The prince's steadfast eyes were a veritable destructive force.

However, Agata was no pushover either. Refusing to be taken for a greenhorn, he calmly stared back.

"…Okay," Wein answered finally. "If you promise to honor our trade deal, I guess I can cooperate."

"Of course. I guarantee you'll reap great rewards."

"It's decided, then."

Wein and Agata shook hands, forming a secret pact between the two great rivals.

Then—

"Yep, I'm gonna backstab Agata."

"What?"

Once the two were back in the carriage, Wein revealed his intentions to Ninym and her eyes went wide.

As several political schemes gripped the Ulbeth Alliance, an outsider arrived. Wein would rise to the stage, and the land would descend into chaos.

"Uhh…" Wein and company were back at the temporary residence the Ulbeth Alliance had set up for them. The prince was groaning with unease. "This mask *protects* your household…?"

The object in Wein's hands was a common sort of handicraft that could be found on sale throughout the region, and he'd purchased several on a whim.

"It does look more like something you'd wear to scare off enemies," Ninym replied as she took it from him.

"Or freak out little kids."

"I think that kind of reaction is the point. It's proof of its effectiveness, you could say. It's not happening right now, but I heard there's a festival where everyone parades around town in masks like these."

Wein imagined a sea of terrifying crafted faces marching through the dark night and shivered. The celebration sounded like a nightmare for children and uninformed adults alike.

"I also recall that there's a masked gathering where people can vent their various frustrations."

"Makes sense to me. The Ulbeth government keeps tabs on everyone. I guess a masquerade party helps them cope."

"It's an established custom, so authorities usually look the other way," Ninym added. She then donned the mask. "'I serve a certain noble, but he's an awful troublemaker...' Just kidding."

Wein laughed. "Who could you be referring to? He sounds like a handful."

"Care to try it on, Wein?" Ninym giggled.

However, the prince swept his hair back theatrically. "Don't need it. Concealing these good looks would be a disservice to the continent!"

"..."

"..."

Ninym quietly held the mask over her face again. "Well then, I have work to do."

"Wait! Don't ignore me, Miss Ninym...! It hurts my feelings...!"

"Ninym? I, the Masked Flahmette, am a simple passerby."

"My subordinate is in a *super* bad mood! What should I do, O adorable Masked Flahmette?!"

"She'll feel much better if you devote yourself to your job and don't spout nonsense." Ninym, aka the Masked Flahmette, set documents in front of the crestfallen Wein. "First, let's review the situation. We want to make a trade deal with Ulbeth, right? Commerce between Natra and Patura took a significant hit, so we'll need a substitute."

"Right. We trekked here from the far north to help Agata with his scheme in exchange for a business deal," Wein responded, his previous despair now gone. "But after seeing things for myself, it's obvious that the situation is quite different from what we assumed. I know each city possesses equal authority, but Agata is a Holy Elite and the public face of the whole nation. I figured he'd at least be a cut above the rest."

"From what we've heard, that's not the case at all," Ninym agreed before cocking her head to one side. "Do foreign entities like Levetia lack influence here because the Ulbeth Alliance is focused on its own strength?"

"Let's worry about the reason later. Right now, our biggest problem is Agata's limited power. It could sink our trade deal."

Agata wanted to unite the four city-states under his own banner, and a trade deal with Natra was plausible if he succeeded. However, Wein and Agata's secret pact would collapse if this plan failed. It all hinged on whether the older man actually brought Ulbeth under his control.

"Man, I was really hoping this would go better."

Wein had, of course, weighed the risks before the trip. He'd supposed that his odds against Agata were pretty good. Even if he did lose by some odd chance, the prince thought he'd at least bring home a consolation prize.

Once Wein had arrived in Muldu, however, he realized that Agata's predicament was worse than he'd imagined. He could already sense this was a colossal waste of time.

"And that's why you're betraying him, right?"

"You got it."

Aiding Agata in bringing the Alliance together wasn't Wein's only option. So long as he achieved his own goal, Ulbeth's unification (or lack thereof) made no difference to Natra's future. Wein already saw an obvious second route.

"We'll try Roynock to the west," he began. "It dominates Ulbeth's sea trade, and we can ditch Agata if I strike a deal with its representative."

Ninym nodded. "Yes, but I have several concerns. First, you'll immediately make an enemy of Agata."

"True, but I doubt he'll be much of a threat. After all, he invited a foreign power like me to help with Ulbeth's domestic issues. If I cut ties with him, a political war against the west and the south will swiftly end his career."

Agata was old, so making a comeback wouldn't be easy. And without authority, no amount of hatred could threaten Wein.

"All right, let's move on. How do you plan to negotiate with Roynock's representative? The Ulbeth Alliance has rejected your business proposal once before."

After Natra had gained access to Soljest's port, Wein immediately solicited every nation along the West's coastline with a trade deal. Unfortunately, his notorious reputation preceded him, leaving other countries wary. Everyone ignored him, including the Ulbeth Alliance, whose naval liaison was, of course, Roynock.

"We won't know until we try, but I think we stand a chance. A lot has changed in the West since then."

"Okay, here's my third and final concern. I know you're going to meet the representative in Roynock, but Agata's involvement worries me."

"Yeah, there's that," Wein groaned. Agata was sharpening the ax for his own demise. It was unnerving, to say the least. "I'm sure he knows I might betray him. Shouldn't that make him nervous about leaving me alone with the West and the South Representatives?"

"Yet he's prepared that exact scenario. Agata might believe you can't betray him, and perhaps his confidence is warranted. We should be careful," said Ninym.

"Right. And there's something else that bothers me."

"Something else?" Not sure what other points she missed, Ninym gave Wein a puzzled look.

"I'm not sure…how serious Agata is about unification."

Ninym's visible confusion grew deeper. "From what we know, Agata's political position is slowly declining. Asking a foreign power for aid seems genuine to me."

Agata had dragged Wein into the fray because Roynock and Facrita overshadowed Muldu. Such was the present situation.

"Still, Agata's heart doesn't seem in it."

A seat of authority was a wondrous thing. Almost every leader, even the most composed, would fight to the death to guard their power.

Wein didn't sense this from Agata, however. The Holy Elite asserted that his goal was unification, but it felt like the man was running in a different lane.

"What other objective could he have?"

"No clue," Wein replied blankly.

"I suppose it *is* a bit early to say."

They'd already learned a lot in this city, but there were still plenty of unknowns. Blindly guessing Agata's motive wouldn't accomplish much. They needed information.

"Well, no use worrying. Let's set that aside for now and get ready for the banquet."

"Right. I'll also gather more details about the Alliance." Ninym paused to let out a sigh. "I wish I could come with you, but as your aide, I know that associating with me would damage your reputation. Even if my hair is dyed, a Flahm like me should remain in the background."

"Come to think of it, didn't you mention that the aide from earlier realized you're a Flahm? What was his name... Kamil, right?"

"Yes, but fortunately, he doesn't seem prejudiced."

Ninym shrugged but found no reason to celebrate. If Kamil had said something cruel, there would have been bloodshed once

Wein found out. To her immense relief, their conversation had been unremarkable.

"Perhaps he's a rare exception. Then again, Levetia's influence is shaky here, so maybe people in the Ulbeth Alliance are more accepting of the Flahm?"

"Even so, let's not test that theory."

Taking such risks despite full knowledge of Wein's imperial wrath was suicidal. Ninym didn't want Ulbeth reduced to ash.

"Besides, Flahm prejudice or not, the Alliance clearly despises outsiders."

She could still feel those penetrating eyes as the carriage traveled through the city. The heavy, insular atmosphere was hardly inviting.

"Well, let's meet up with the West Representative first and try to work out a deal. That'll decide whether or not we betray Agata."

"Let me say this first—be *very* careful. Don't cause unnecessary trouble."

Wein grinned. "Better hope peace loves me."

Ninym let out a defeated sigh. "…I'll prepare an escape route."

"Good morning, Prince Wein."

On the day of the banquet, Agata's aide, Kamil, met the foreign delegation outside of their provided accommodation.

"Master Agata has instructed me to escort you to the venue."

"Thanks. I don't really know my way around town yet."

Kamil bowed courteously. "We can depart at your earliest convenience. Is that all right?"

"Sure, sounds good. Let's get going." Wein nodded before

turning to Ninym behind him. "Well, I'm off. Hold down the fort while I'm gone."

"Yes. Please take care, Your Highness."

Ninym watched Wein and Kamil's carriage depart.

"By the way, what's the occasion?"

"The children of two influential people, one from Roynock and the other from Facrita, are getting married. The West Representative is hosting the affair since the groom-to-be is his close relative."

"I see. How wonderful," Wein replied before asking a follow-up question. "Shouldn't the party be in Roynock, then?"

"Although I believe the engagement is a political bargain between the west and the south, the location was likely chosen because the West Representative's relative lives in Muldu."

"Traveling all the way here for a family engagement? That's rough."

"The four cities have upheld a policy of appeasement since the Alliance's founding, so most people have relatives throughout Ulbeth. Traveling between cities to attend a wedding is quite common."

"Oh yeah? You make it sound as though Ulbeth has a firm sense of solidarity."

"If only it were that simple." Kamil let out a heavy sigh. "We've laid a solid foundation and can handle foreign nations, thanks to the appeasement policy, but the rivalry between the cities is rising drastically. Each of the four believes itself the true leader of the union. Politicians have even tried to gain the upper hand by inciting their own citizens. Unfortunately, this has also opened old wounds."

Mutual encouragement through healthy rivalry could nurture

cultures, ideas, and techniques. However, the relationship quickly soured when anger and resentment were thrown into the mix.

"I know those types. Higher-ups that engage in that kind of manipulation are especially annoying."

"I must agree, Prince."

Wein and Kamil smiled wryly at each other.

Those who managed their own domains regularly took to thinking half the city and even the entire nation belonged to them. They gleefully snatched up all the credit when their settlement prospered yet panicked more than anyone once things turned bleak. It wasn't too dire an issue in moderation, but this could rapidly go belly-up if the situation turned extreme.

"The marriage of a relative is paramount to such people. After all, someone you dislike may suddenly become close family."

"It must be tough to balance feelings and profit."

"Indeed. The familial relationships in Ulbeth are a complex labyrinth. Even today's couple argued bitterly and nearly broken off their engagement, but the West and the South Representatives managed to keep them together."

The carriage arrived at the mansion while Wein and Kamil conversed. Other guests had already gathered, and there seemed to be a large crowd inside.

"You know, Prince Wein, disjointed as they are, the Ulbeth people transform when a certain something is in their midst. Do you know what that is?"

"A foreigner, right?"

Kamil only smiled, and the two entered the building. The mood changed instantly.

"My, what an auspicious day."

"Indeed. The weather is crisp and clear."

The reception hall was vast enough to accommodate a large crowd, and guests filled every corner, chatting all the while. The light tone matched the joyous occasion, but their comments were less than complimentary.

"Ha-ha-ha, this fresh air is more than the weather."

"Oh…? Why, you're right. Those dirty easterners aren't here, are they?"

"No, look over there. They're skulking in the corner."

"Heh. How impressive for a group that boasts only arrogance."

"I do wish they'd realize their star has fallen."

"Why, I'm certain they'll understand once we demonstrate Roynock and Facrita's unbreakable bond."

The gossipers sneered openly as their targets, those guests from Muldu, silently endured the abuse.

Harsh…

Despite the engagement party being held in the eastern city, the locals were being dragged through the mud. It underlined just how much Roynock and Facrita despised them.

Still, it looks like Muldu might have a chance to turn things around.

A quick glance revealed that most of the attendees were from Roynock or Facrita. The Muldu guests were a small minority. What's more, there weren't any guests from Altie. Invitees from the west and the south patted themselves on the back and acted as if their friendship were forever, but that glint in their eyes revealed both factions considered the other to be a nuisance. It was obvious that, given half a chance, they would be at each other's throats.

They'll settle down soon enough, though.

After all, Wein—a foreigner—was now in their midst.

"Hey, who's that?"

"That's one of Agata's men with him."

"Wait, could it be the visitor from Natra?"

"You mean Natra's crown prince?!"

The stares and whispers escalated as Wein moved into the center of the room. The distrust and suspicion were almost palpable. It was hardly a warm welcome.

"What did the prince come to Ulbeth for…?"

"I heard his mind is a steel trap. He's definitely up to something."

"Sir Agata invited him, right? Does that mean Natra is allies with the eastern city?"

"If so, that makes him an enemy…"

Animosity flooded the hall. Even Kamil, who was only a guide, looked tense. Had the glares from the crowd been solid arrows, Wein would have resembled a hedgehog by now.

Naturally, the prince wasn't the least bit intimidated. His arrogant smile practically declared him king.

"He is over there, Prince Wein."

"So that's the West Representative I've heard so much about?"

Kamil directed Wein's attention to a man slightly older than the prince. He was Oleom, the young genius and the representative of Roynock.

"It has been some time, Sir Oleom." Kamil stopped and gave a polite bow.

"Indeed it has, Kamil," Oleom replied in a slow, cautious tone. He knew Kamil was Agata's aide. "I'm pleased to see you in good health. How is Sir Agata?"

"Quite well. Thankfully, he is as fit as ever."

"I'm glad to hear it. However, I don't recall inviting you today."

"Yes, about that… I hastened here because I wish to introduce an individual quite suited to this honored occasion."

With a look from Kamil, Wein stepped forward.

"I'm the crown prince of Natra, Wein Salema Arbalest. It's a pleasure to meet you, West Representative Oleom."

Wein greeted the other man courteously while taking in his every move. What would the response be?

"Oh my," Oleom said with a mellow smile. "I am Oleom, Roynock's West Representative. It is an honor to meet you, Prince Wein. I have heard many rumors."

"Rumors? How embarrassing to hear my name has reached as far as Ulbeth. I hope they're all flattering."

"I daresay everyone has heard of the Dragon of the North. You have achieved much despite your youth, Prince Wein. I must follow your example."

"Is that so? I'll have to work harder or risk shattering my image."

Wein and Oleom exchanged warm expressions, and their conversation was civil. However, every spectator understood that Oleom's comments were layered with insults. Naturally, Wein recognized this, too, but said nothing. His grin only deepened as things continued.

"You're young as well, Sir Oleom. I had assumed all representatives were up in years like Agata."

"I inherited the title several years ago after my aging predecessor could no longer fulfill his duties. This has made garnering respect difficult," Oleom explained. "However, compared to the woman approaching us, my presence is a mild breeze."

Wein followed Oleom's gaze and looked over his shoulder at the lady sauntering closer.

"Lejoutte, this is—"

"I know." She cut Oleom off and addressed Wein directly. "It's nice to meet you, Prince Wein. I'm Lejoutte, the South Representative."

Lejoutte was around Oleom's age. In other words, someone who would typically have been too inexperienced to lead a city of tens of thousands.

"…Did Facrita have a recent change in power as well?"

"Yes. She was appointed around the same time," Oleom answered.

"I see." Wein nodded. "You *do* have it hard."

"Right?"

"What are you two talking about?"

"Only the great responsibility we bear, Lejoutte." Oleom shrugged, and his fellow representative glared at him suspiciously for a moment before finally shifting her attention to Wein.

"Well, no matter. Prince Wein, I'll get right to the point. Why have you come here? I must assume congratulating a couple over their engagement isn't your only motivation." Unlike Oleom, Lejoutte ditched subtle disdain and went straight for the jugular. Her crossed arms and sharp glare made it clear she had no intention of getting along.

"And if I claimed that truly is the only reason?" Wein questioned with an even tone. "Truth is, I love celebrating others' happiness. In my country, I'm called 'The Matchmaker Prince.' Whenever there's a new engagement announcement or wedding, I'm there in a heartbeat."

Lejoutte couldn't hide a grimace as Wein lied through his teeth. Oleom gave an entertained chuckle.

"How very generous. I'm certain the couple will consider your blessings a lifelong honor."

"You actually *believe* him? How can you joke when people claim this prince started the recent famine?"

"…Sir Oleom, I thought you said all the rumors were positive?"

"I think even infamy has its own prestige," Oleom deflected.

Wein sniffed in amusement, and Oleom looked at Lejoutte as he continued, "No one can create an artificial famine. It's impractical, not to mention heartless. Even if such methods did exist, the culprit would have to be a cold-blooded monster."

"Or an evil dragon."

"Oh dear. In that case, you'd better watch out. Your very bones will be charred if you're not careful."

Wein and Oleom laughed. It was a dry, disturbing sound.

"…This is a waste of time," Lejoutte groaned, as if hoping to change the subject. "There's nothing worse than watching two men bicker pointlessly. Prince Wein, I will leave if you insist on keeping up this charade."

"It's no charade. As I said, I'm here to offer my congratulations."

"Is that so? Then perhaps you could pass on a message to Agata for me: 'It doesn't matter what tricks you pull. Your era is over. From now on, Facrita will be the heart of the Ulbeth Alliance.'"

Turning on her heel, Lejoutte exited as boldly as she'd come. Oleom watched her proud figure recede and shrugged. "Goodness, what discourteous behavior toward a crown prince. She's always been a bit headstrong. I do hope you'll consider it part of her charm."

"No offense taken. But do you agree with that last statement, Sir Oleom?"

"Hardly," he admitted with a chuckle. "Roynock will be the center of the next era. Well then, I must greet the other guests, so if you'll excuse me. Please enjoy the party, Prince Wein."

Oleom took his leave.

"'Get a sense of their characters,' huh?"

Wein looked around him. No one had admonished the representatives for disrespecting a foreign prince. In fact, those whispering seemed to sympathize with them.

"I'm terribly sorry, Prince Wein. I never imagined they'd act so brazen…" Kamil apologized after having silently observed the exchange. His position kept him from interfering, but his face had paled at the discourteousness shown to a visiting dignitary.

Wein himself remained unbothered, however.

"Don't worry about it. I couldn't handle foreign diplomacy if I let something like this get to me. Plus, imagine if I were the moody type."

"What…?"

Kamil blinked in confusion, but Wein ignored it and carried on.

"Anyway, we're here now. I better rub elbows with more than just the representatives. Kamil, find me a good candidate."

"Y-yes. Understood."

Still baffled, Kamil did as ordered. Wein formulated his next plan in the meantime.

In the White Willow of Muldu, Ninym sighed as she walked down a deserted alley.

As I thought, the city's layout is almost identical to Lushan's, but…

Most Western cities were modeled after Levetia's stronghold, Lushan. This was a testament to both the old capital's degree of perfection and Levetia's influence. Muldu was no exception, and much of it resembled what Ninym recalled from Wein's earlier visit to the capital. The atmosphere was markedly different, though.

It's suffocating.

This was Ninym's honest opinion after exploring more of the city.

As Levetia's home base, Lushan had a solemn air that some could find oppressive. Muldu had a tenseness, too, yet it lacked divinity. The climate felt more like a turf war between beasts.

I guess this is another evil of the Ulbeth Alliance.

While not official, Muldu was effectively divided into a few districts. There was one for merchants, one for craftsmen, and one for leaders and the nobility.

Every city in Ulbeth was demarcated, but the distinction was particularly noticeable in Muldu. Each section had its own rules, and any outside presence was highly frowned upon. Therefore, the locals' talent for spotting strangers was keen, and Ninym drew looks everywhere she went. Nothing could be more troublesome for a person who wished to stay in the shadows.

At least it was worth it.

Through inquiry and investigation, she gathered helpful information about the Ulbeth Alliance, Muldu, and Agata. She'd share it with Wein later.

Lost in thought, Ninym was heading back to the mansion when…

…she saw someone standing in the road ahead.

"_____"

A part of her had been hoping not to.

After noticing Kamil's tolerance, Ninym realized the Alliance and Lushan were similar but not identical. She'd wondered if, like Patura to the south, Ulbeth was a unique Western culture untainted by Levetia's influence. The simple fact that Ninym hadn't come across any Flahm thus far allowed her to believe that her kin were happy here.

Unsurprisingly, that was *not the case.*

"Ah…"

Ninym instinctively looked down, but the sight was already burned into her mind.

A man in tattered clothes was carrying a heavy load. There were shackles around his feet. His eyes sparkled like crimson jewels, and his hair was a pale white.

There could be no mistaking it. He was a slave—a Flahm slave.

Calm down. This is common in the West. Ninym pressed a hand to her racing heart.

The Flahm man known as the Founder had created a nation for his oppressed and enslaved people. However, their kingdom was destroyed, and the Flahm were persecuted yet again, even worse than before.

Still, the Flahm weren't the only victims of slavery. Every era demanded cheap labor. Whether victims of war, flesh hunters, or someone else's financial greed, people were cast into bondage for various reasons.

That's why this isn't a big deal. No need to get emotional. Return to the mansion. Hurry.

Ninym was a Flahm, but she also served Natra's royal family. The nation came first. Stirring up drama with slaves while abroad would only trouble Wein. And so the young woman told herself to leave.

Yet her body refused to move. Before she knew it, Ninym was peering straight ahead.

"Ah…"

The Flahm man was still there. And he was staring right at her.

An instinctual sort of chill ran through Ninym. It didn't matter if her hair was dyed black. He knew she was a Flahm.

This is bad. Run away. I can't cause Wein trouble, but—

The conflict between Ninym's mind and body left her frozen.

©Falmaro

Had they been gazing at each other for a few seconds or a few minutes? As she sank into endless agony, the Flahm man flashed her a troubled look.

"Heh."

Then he smiled.

It was tiny yet filled with compassion.

What was the meaning behind it? Before Ninym could ask, the slave departed as if nothing had happened.

Shocked and breathless, Ninym stood alone for a long time.

"—And that's what happened."

Wein had explained the events of the party to Ninym in private.

"It looks like Oleom and Lejoutte are convinced I support Muldu, so it'll be hard to team up with Facrita or Roynock. I suppose I can understand avoiding foreign aid when it still appears you can win on your own."

"..."

"Still, there are definitely cracks forming between them. They might be friends now, but they'll be ready to butt heads once Muldu is out of the picture."

"..."

"Ninym?"

The young woman jolted. "Ah, s-sorry. I was just thinking."

Wein fell silent for a moment, then looked deep into Ninym's eyes.

"Ninym, I'm only going to ask once... Is something wrong?"

"No, it's fine," she asserted.

Wein closed his eyes and seemed to ruminate over her answer.

"Okay," he said with a slight nod. "In that case, let's plan our next steps."

Aware he was being considerate, Ninym did her best to focus.

"Agata will be our only option if we can't negotiate with the Roynock or Facrita, right?"

"Yeah, most likely. Agata must have sent me to the party because he saw this coming," Wein replied, obviously irritated. Regardless of whether Agata's motive for aiding the enemy was a mystery, Wein had greatly underestimated the chance of failed negotiations. "I do have another idea, however."

"What is it?"

"We'll keep helping Agata, but half-ass it. Once he's down for the count, we can join either the western or the southern city when they start fighting each other."

For Wein, Agata's victory was convenient but hardly a requirement. The Roynock-Facrita partnership would end with the representative of Muldu's defeat, and Natra's foreign military would make a tempting ally when Roynock and Facrita went to war.

"Still, this plan has its flaws," Wein admitted.

"It'll take time."

"Yep." The prince groaned. "We can only make a deal once Agata is out of the way and those two turn on each other. If we're not careful, we'll be stuck here 'til spring."

"We shouldn't be gone from Natra for too long. There's plenty to be done back home."

"So I'm not allowed to procrastinate if I stay in Ulbeth?"

"This isn't a vacation."

"Can't argue with that," Wein replied. Then he muttered, "Still, Sirgis is easier to maneuver when I'm away."

"Did you say something?"

"Nope. Hey, who else is hungry?"

"I'll prepare something after our discussion," Ninym answered before returning to the conversation at hand. "Regardless of time limits, I'm not sure you'll be able to negotiate. From what you've told me, they don't sound like your biggest fans. I also felt this nation's deep-rooted bigotry while exploring the city."

"Oh, I wouldn't worry about that."

"Why?"

Wein smirked. "You might say it's the fate of every young politician."

"Welcome back, Lady Lejoutte."

The representative of Facrita's subordinates politely greeted her as she returned to her temporary residence in Muldu.

"How was the celebration?"

"It went well. Agata sent Natra's crown prince to meddle in the affairs, but it was a meaningless effort. Muldu *will* fall."

"You are as brilliant as ever, Lady Lejoutte."

"Facrita is in excellent hands."

"Isn't Natra some remote northern country? What could their prince ever accomplish?"

"I couldn't agree more. Besides, Sir Agata is just a senile old man."

"At this rate, that newcomer Oleom will fall as well. The southern city will soon rule the Alliance…!"

Lejoutte threw a sidelong glance at her enthusiastic followers and quietly sighed. "I'd like a moment to think. I'll be in my room, so do not disturb me."

"Yes, understood."

They bade her farewell, and Lejoutte returned to her quarters. Then—

"SHOOOOOOOOOOOOT!"

She crouched down with her head in her hands.

"WHY?! Why did Natra's prince have to show up *now*?!"

Lejoutte cast off her noble air and pummeled the bed next to her.

"If he'd come just a little sooner or later, I could have convinced everyone our partnership is a good idea…!"

Brave young Lejoutte was the South Representative. Her pedigree was, of course, impeccable, and she demonstrated promising talent as well. In her pre-representative career, she had focused on improving inefficient agricultural techniques by visiting local farmlands, actively conversing with staff, and rewarding ingenuity. Lejoutte integrated foreign expertise as well. To the small-minded Ulbeth people, her methods were highly irregular.

Naturally, there were critics, but the results silenced them. The produce output in her domain soared, and others tried to imitate her success. Keeping no secrets, Lejoutte openly shared her agricultural techniques. Altie prospered even further, and Lejoutte was appointed representative.

In this new position, she immediately allied with the naval city of Roynock to the west and used this new market outlet to great success.

"I've worked so hard. My position should be solid…but I suppose that's too much to ask."

Lejoutte sighed in exasperation. Her youth made people underestimate her, but there was also the matter of her agricultural innovations. Those who benefited were ecstatic, yet it was not a unanimous victory. Some were even left at a disadvantage, and they saw Lejoutte as a bitter enemy. This was where Ulbeth's complex family tree came into play. The disgruntled tried to tarnish her by complaining among their own circles.

Altie's relationship with Roynock was limited as well. The Ulbeth Alliance was formed of four cities that allegedly held equal power, but in truth, each citizen considered their city above the rest. While Altie flourished, thanks to its cooperation with Roynock, everyone irritably thought, *"They should be bowing to* us. *Now we look like equals or something."*

"You're all so stupid, stupid, stupid…!"

Now Lejoutte had to make Ulbeth and the rest of the continent believe she had befriended Roynock out of necessity and would eventually abandon them. Anything else would cost the woman her representative position.

"Why is nothing working out…?!"

Lejoutte could have made a deal with Natra had she not already sided with Roynock or cut ties already. That opportunity was long gone, however. Altie was more confident than ever before. Lejoutte had been forced to snub Wein at the party lest she appear weak and timid.

"Hahhh… Oh, Oleom… What should I do…?" Lejoutte whispered into the air.

There are jokes about every nation.

Why is there no face powder in Natra? Because it's piled up outside!

Why are there no plates in Soljest? Because they were eaten!

And…

Why are there no world maps in the Ulbeth Alliance? Because the people insist they're at the center!

"…At the end of the day, we're bumpkins in denial."

In his private quarters, West Representative Oleom was mumbling to himself.

The Ulbeth Alliance was a union among four city-states that had once battled for hegemony of their region. It wasn't a large area in any respect. Ulbeth mocked Natra as the "northern backwoods," but other countries regarded Ulbeth as the "western boonies." What's more, Natra was a rising world superpower. Oleom doubted Ulbeth could keep up.

"Location aside, it was a mistake to leave Muldu in charge of foreign affairs."

The four remote cities created two policies when they'd founded the Alliance.

First, each city would develop its specialized industry and compensate for the others' shortcomings. This would ensure an efficient government.

Second, all the settlements were to keep their competitive spirit alive while maintaining harmony and encouraging one another.

"I don't think those policies were a mistake, but…"

So much time had passed that everyone had lost sight of the original aim of the two tenets.

People failed to hone their strengths and forgot anything that wasn't their one job. They were glad to leave unpleasant tasks to their neighbors, but the mutual hostility within the Ulbeth Alliance never faded.

Although foolish, many citizens thought the following despite their own city's incompetence: *Other cities can handle the annoying stuff. Ours should rule the Alliance anyway.*

"If only we could have resolved things and maintained the union.

Yet Facrita and Roynock are making rapid progress, and Muldu is failing..."

The southern and the western cities were excited to become the face of Ulbeth. However, people failed to realize that they would be taking over Muldu's diplomatic duties. The uneducated and xenophobic Ulbethians would have to carry the torch.

Pointing this out wouldn't do much good either. Since citizens respected only their own city, most would laugh off the danger and say, *"The others can handle it, right?"*

"People understand the risk of allowing an amateur to do a master's work when it's their own field yet optimistically believe everything will work out somehow when those roles are reversed. Maybe that's human nature."

Oleom's mouth twisted into a sardonic expression.

He had a duty to lead Roynock as West Representative. It was a frustrating job, though, and Wein's appearance at the banquet was a perfect example. Befriending the prince was obviously the best option, but Oleom's citizens would never approve. After all, they believed themselves superior and didn't understand Natra's importance.

"Lejoutte...what should I do...?"

The man's anguished whispers went unheard.

"I see. So civic duty shaped their reactions rather than personal feelings." Ninym nodded after hearing Wein's explanation. "I also heard that both representatives were only appointed a few years ago. It's no surprise things are troubled when they don't have a strong grip on their factions yet."

Both Oleom and Lejoutte were regularly praised for their competence, yet neither had unanimous support.

This seamless transition of power to a talented new generation would have made the Empire's people grit their teeth and say, *How nice for you.*

"Wow, those two really do have it rough. I can relate," Wein remarked. As another bright, young leader of tomorrow, he could easily sympathize.

"So will you show mercy and go easy on them?"

"What? Nah."

And there you have it.

"I'm a man who can separate his work and personal life, after all."

"I suppose I can't complain about that." Ninym wasn't totally satisfied with the prince's answer but moved on anyway. "At any rate, I understand now that there is still opportunity for negotiation. What are your plans, though? Should we prepare for a long battle?"

"Hmm..."

Wein pondered for a while. It was a rare sight since he usually went with his gut or devised a quick solution despite potential concerns. Were the scales tipped so evenly, showing no favor for one option over the other?

"Okay. We'll meet Agata tomorrow, hear him out, and go from there," Wein decided after much deliberation. "If he just wants to break up Facrita and Roynock's honeymoon, we'll cut ties right there and join the southern city or the western one."

"Sounds reasonable," Ninym replied, nodding. "But we should also consider retreat if it looks like this will take too long."

"No way. I'm not going home empty-handed."

"Sometimes it's important to cut your losses."

"We'll cross that bridge when we come to it. Yup, just leave everything to me."

Wein was brimming with confidence, but Ninym had to wonder if they'd truly be all right.

The next day, Wein met Agata at the Holy Elite's mansion.

"So what did you think of Oleom and Lejoutte?" Agata inquired shamelessly.

Ninym kept her scowl hidden from her place behind Wein. Last time, she'd had to wait in a separate room, but Agata and his aide Kamil didn't mind that Ninym was a Flahm and allowed her to join Wein during this meeting. Even so, she had no authority to speak and thus could only observe.

"They were quite delightful. Given time to mature, Ulbeth will be in excellent hands," Wein replied cheerfully. His comments were dripping with sarcasm, but Agata wouldn't have become East Representative without a thick skin.

"Exactly. That's why I must stop them."

"Got any ideas?"

"This." Agata had Kamil bring over a large stack of papers. "I have gathered various records about Ulbeth's citizens over my long career as East Representative. No other city has such a vast collection. I will use this to divide Roynock and Facrita. I want your help in convincing others to join our cause, Prince Wein."

Ah, this is never going to work, Ninym thought immediately.

The volume of information was impressive, but it was your run-of-the-mill scheme from every angle. Based on what Wein had told Ninym the night before, he intended to end things with Agata now and join Roynock or Facrita. She couldn't see the prince's expression from behind him, but she imagined he looked bored to tears.

However, Ninym couldn't have been more wrong.

What's going on?

Wein stared Agata dead in the eye. He had a vague sense of the man's intentions.

Agata wants to drag this out. And he's totally fine with me joining the south or the west to make it happen...!

There was no proof, but Wein knew. The stone-faced Agata's crumb trail of information led him to this conclusion. It was undeniable. This gave rise to another concern, however.

The unification is a bluff, and the homewrecker plan is, too. In fact, he doesn't even want to be representative...! Sending me to that party was supposed to trick me into believing I had leeway to team up with Roynock or Facrita. Agata is making every excuse to keep me here! But why?

Wein couldn't read him. Agata's deepest core was shrouded. Still, even if he didn't know what the Holy Elite was thinking, there was something the prince did understand.

This was a trap—an extremely convoluted one.

Knowing this, Wein...

Interesting. Okay, let's dance, Agata!

...felt an excited flame burn in his chest.

"...What an impressive collection. I'd expect no less from Muldu's veteran representative. Clearly, you have nothing to worry about with these in hand." Wein began to test the waters. "Still, Sir Agata, I wonder if you're being a bit light-handed."

"Oh...?" Agata's eyes flashed with evident interest. "Are you suggesting I use greater force? The Ulbeth Alliance usually avoids such measures, but…"

"Not at all. Anyone who has records like these but chooses violence should return to the pack of monkeys they clearly belong to. I have a more constructive way to split the opposition."

Wein's thoughts whirled excitedly.

I see your game, Agata. You want me to stick around here. In that case, I'll do the complete opposite! I'm gonna wrap things up pronto and hightail it out of Ulbeth!

A dazzling smile spread across the prince of Natra's face.

"In other words—it's time for a marriage campaign."

Cedric was the son of a small-time Muldu merchant. He was young, healthy, and even possessed a bit of business sense. He expected to inherit his father's shop one day and didn't need to look on the bright side to see life was coming up roses.

There was something that concerned him, however. Despite coming of age some time ago, he was still unmarried.

"Well, that's pretty common in Ulbeth…," Cedric mumbled while minding the store.

Thanks to their nation's long history, family ties in Ulbeth were far-reaching. Of course, the term "relative" was all subjective, but there were plenty of fish in the sea when hunting for a good partner.

In Ulbeth, marriage was a huge hassle.

First, once you found a possible match, you had to investigate the person's hometown, lineage, and personal history. You also had to confirm that their close relatives weren't business rivals or other hostile parties.

Next came ensuring that marriage to this person wouldn't cause drama among your own kin. You were golden if everything checked out, but Ulbeth's interwoven families inevitably meant some relatives refused to give their blessing. If there was too much opposition, the engagement was called off. Should compromise appear possible, you did your best to persuade the naysayers. If your potential partner managed to overcome those same obstacles, the two of you could openly discuss marriage.

Frankly, it was one immense pain.

"Count me out..."

Cedric spoke for most Ulbethians his age. Most thought, *It's so stupid. Why bother?*

Regardless, they couldn't voice such opinions in Ulbeth society. Loose lips were immediately ostracized, as countless past examples proved. When someone publicly advocated free love and the abolition of marriage protocol, even Cedric had to mock their "selfishness" out of peer pressure and jealousy.

"*Hahhh...* Can someone please just destroy us already?"

Cedric viewed Ulbeth like a tight ball of string. It was the nation's own handiwork, but the threads slowly suffocating them could no longer be unwound by human hands. If only someone would come and crush everything—

"Hey, Cedric!"

"Huh?"

His father had come bursting through the door.

"What's wrong, Dad?"

The moment Cedric asked, he saw his father's expression and realized it was urgent news. Just as he was wondering if the store had made an amazing deal—

"Rejoice! You have a marriage interview!"

—Cedric fell off his chair.

"...The Houdard and Juino families are discussing a possible union?"

Lejoutte frowned at this unexpected report from her subordinate. "That's odd. Although both families have children around the same age, they're on poor terms."

"I thought it strange as well and checked the information, but it appears to be accurate. Nothing's set in stone yet, however."

"Hmm..."

Lejoutte fell silent for a moment. The news was surprising, but she was more baffled that this development hadn't reached her ears more swiftly. The Ulbeth Alliance was a mass surveillance society. If someone was causing problems, government leaders—Lejoutte included—would hear about it.

Houdard's a Muldu family with a social standing that rivals Agata's, but the Juinos are from Altie... Did Agata purposefully keep this plan under wraps?

Attracting as many people as possible was a vital skill for any leader, but in a closed society like the Ulbeth Alliance, poaching human resources was regular. Whenever it looked like a marriage might rob a city of its valued member, leaders tried to stop the union. This made it even more challenging for young Ulbethians to get married, and factions preferred to keep weddings within their own established circles.

"I suppose it's inconsequential, though. This will have no impact on us."

Lejoutte felt uneasy for some reason, but she brushed the feeling aside. The woman wouldn't hesitate to intervene as needed, yet such actions garnered enmity if done too regularly. Politicians had to choose their battles wisely.

"We'll be sure to congratulate them. Send someone as my proxy."

"Pardon me!"

Another subordinate hurried into the room.

"The head of the Ramanuchin family has arrived! He requests an audience with you, Lady Lejoutte!"

"What? The Ramanuchin family? I have no plans to meet with them today."

"Yes, but he would like your approval for a marriage between their eldest son and the eldest daughter of the Melmet family..."

The color drained from Lejoutte's face.

"Wasn't he supposed to marry the second daughter of Balash family from Facrita?!"

The Ramanuchins were different from the Houdards and the Juinos. Although on the fringes, they were unquestionably part of Lejoutte's faction.

Yet they want to marry into the Melmet family?! They're from Muldu!

Lejoutte quickly began to seethe at this outrageous betrayal but calmed herself with logic. Acting disagreeable here wouldn't do. She had to deduce how this situation had come about in the first place.

"I'll be right there. Where is the family head?"

"In the reception room."

Lejoutte promptly readied herself and set out to meet him.

They're free to betray Facrita. The Ramanuchins are outliers, after all. I can readily oust them if need be. Still, I'm surprised I didn't discover their dealings with the Melmet family earlier. Even if they were acting covertly, that only gets you so far. Plus, they were discussing marriage of all things!

Wedding arrangements in the Ulbeth Alliance were long-winded due to an ongoing settlement of interests. No matter how one tried to keep the matter quiet, it would inevitably leak somewhere. Yet somehow, Lejoutte had been entirely ignorant of these affairs. What was going on?

Can I brush off two marriage talks with Muldu families as mere coincidence? Absolutely not!

This was more than happenstance. It was undeniably an attack meant to undermine the eastern city's opposition. The methods were inscrutable. How had this not come to light sooner?

No, what if my assumptions are wrong? Lejoutte contemplated the possibility. Before long, the picture began to form.

How had they pulled it off? Could they truly accomplish what no other city had before? If so, then—

"Lady Lejoutte!"

The South Representative was about to enter the reception room when another one of her subordinates approached.

"I have news! The Clyffe family in Muldu and the Behnackel family in Roynock have agreed on an engagement!"

"...!"

Even for the Ulbeth Alliance, the history between those two clans was infamously twisted. Agata and Oleom tried to keep them under control, but both sides were unruly and thus mainly left to their own devices.

A sudden engagement between the Clyffes and the Behnackels... It's hard to believe, but there's no longer any question!

The mastermind behind this hadn't been hiding information. Instead, they had used the precedent of prolonged marriage talks to their advantage and settled matters before the news had time to travel.

Then, the one unraveling Ulbeth's tight knots is—!

In other words, it's like a puzzle piece, Ninym mused.

The Ulbeth Alliance's isolated nature jumbled relationships between friends, relatives, coworkers, and business partners. Each citizen became a complex piece.

Of course, most people didn't jump down each other's throats without reason. That vitriol formed over long years of smaller clashes against one another. It had built up to such a degree that the populace of modern Ulbeth found themselves in hopeless situations more often than most, however.

Only foreigners could ignore the ridiculous situation. Those citizens who were aware of their suffering were still Ulbethians whose lives revolved around their respective cities. They could never look down on their nation's distinct rules. Anyone else was an outsider, had no intention of staying in Ulbeth, didn't respect the local laws, or possessed the ability to send the nation flying.

Wein Salema Arbalest was all of the above.

"We'll set up this family's third son next. Prepare the letter. In the meantime, I'll discuss marriage interviews with some families in Altie, so find a venue for me. We should be able to contact them through the Juinos. Oh, this Roynock guy's the perfect age. I should ask about him, too. Kamil, get me his records."

The marriage campaign was underway.

After Wein had made his declaration, Agata's subordinates went scurrying around following his every command.

Who's the real master of this mansion?

An exasperated Ninym watched Wein issue orders. Her exasperation was understandable. She and the prince were in Agata's mansion, but anyone who beheld this display would conclude that Wein was running the show.

Agata's servants only complied because the East Representative had ordered them to, of course, yet they were fascinated by Wein nonetheless.

Still, his plan is so basic.

Ninym was right; Wein's strategy was finely executed but not very elaborate. The young man had browsed Agata's records, considered each person's situation, and recommended suitable couples. That was it. His precision and speed revealed the true genius behind the tactic, however.

It wasn't as if these bachelors and bachelorettes had chosen the single life. Most had been locked in that position due to one circumstance or another.

Wein hummed a little tune as he saw through these obstacles and formed problem-free pairings.

No one could reproduce such a feat. Even Ninym would have needed a decent amount of time, but Wein had already managed to arrange over thirty interviews using Agata's documents alone. It was like finding a grain of gold on the beach every second.

"You could hang up your crown and play matchmaker," Ninym remarked when she had a moment alone with the prince.

Wein laughed. "I've only had this much luck 'cause the Alliance is starved for marriage."

Weddings were a daunting process in Ulbeth, so people jumped at any opportunity—especially one that fell right into their laps.

"Still, I'm surprised by our success. Did you see that room packed with bridal clothes and props? We're running out of space."

Ceremonies were a crucial part of any wedding, but it would take time for the happy couple to assemble everything on their own. Thus, Wein had procured every conceivably necessary item ahead of time and rented them out.

"Don't you think you're overdoing it? I almost drowned in a sea of dresses when I tried to tidy up."

"Better safe than sorry. I just purchased a bunch rather indiscriminately, so I'm not even sure if they're good or not. Plus, it's good to have a load of extras, just in case. Speaking of which, could you try 'em on for quality assurance?"

"..."

Ninym retrieved a mask she'd seemingly conjured from thin air and put it on.

"Boo."

"Irk!"

Wein groaned as the Masked Flahmette poked him.

"I won't name names, but my master has zero tact."

"Huh? Did I say something wrong?"

"You did."

Wein had evidently messed up somewhere along the way. The prince frowned. "Hmm."

Ninym removed the mask. "I'll pass on the dresses. I'm afraid I won't be able to appreciate my own when the time comes."

"That's the main issue?"

"It is."

"Guess that's that, then," Wein mumbled.

Ninym changed the subject. "By the way, do you really want to strengthen Roynock through weddings?"

"Don't worry. I'm already working on phase two."

Phase two. Ninym had already heard the details.

"For phase one, you'll bolster Muldu's authority by linking suitable families to Agata's faction. And during phase two, you aim to use those connections to set up marriages between Roynock and Facrita. Is that right?"

Wein's relationship with the western and the southern cities of the Ulbeth Alliance had been fragile since the beginning. Thus, his scheme was to encourage unions between Roynock and Facrita and build a base that would allow him to interfere.

Ninym had her doubts, however.

"Success just means reinforcing Roynock and Facrita's bond, though, doesn't it?"

"Yep. That's why we're gonna shake up the power balance," Wein replied. "Lejoutte's grip on her faction is shakier, so any marriage with Roynock is a bonus. As Muldu builds momentum and keeps Facrita on edge, how do you think the latter will feel when the former starts stealing their best and brightest through matrimony?"

"Betrayed. They might even suspect collusion between Muldu and Roynock... The southern city won't be happy, to say the very least."

"After that, I'll boost Muldu's status with nonstop wedding bells while the Roynock-Facrita relationship is on the rocks."

Wein saw the floating puzzle pieces created by the Ulbeth Alliance's dilemma as an untapped gold mine. Other leaders would've treaded lightly. Instead, the prince of Natra intended to flood the game board with his own pawns.

"No one will know friend from foe. Everyone from the average citizen to top leaders will be totally lost."

Ultimately, Wein would create a knotted ball so convoluted and tight that most would have no idea where to start, and only a few leaders would be able to brush along the edges. Even those following Wein's orders didn't have all the details. Only the prince had any hope of unraveling it. Thus...

"I'll make it so only I hold the key to Ulbeth's secrets."

He was going to hurl Ulbeth's gnarled ball into a bleak abyss.

"Agata's plans won't matter when everyone is coming to me for answers. I'll be in charge. That's our end game."

Any other country would have protested to some degree. But not the Ulbeth Alliance. There was a direct link between dissent and ostracism in a surveillance society. The populace followed the rules out of self-preservation, which would in turn force them to kneel before Wein.

"They'll be lost without you..."

"Exactly," Wein, the sole keeper of the key, confirmed brightly. "But it's no skin off my nose!"

And there you have it.

Once the prince was indispensable to the Ulbeth Alliance, he could wreck it to his heart's content and scurry back to Natra at his earliest convenience. As a vassal, Ninym was relieved, but as a human being, she was on the fence.

"We've got a few hurdles to clear first."

"Right. Our most pressing issue is money."

Wein was coaxing potential marriage partners to get hitched through letters and discussion, but that didn't solve all their problems. A few people demanded cash and goods, while others couldn't afford a wedding in the first place. Convincing them would require a lot of capital.

Furthermore, Agata was footing most of the bill since a traveler like Wein didn't have much on him. As much as the prince loved spending other people's funds, this arrangement wouldn't last forever.

"Putting together these interviews is costly. At this rate, even Agata's purse will soon run dry."

"Why stop there? Let's bankrupt him."

It was another person's wallet, after all.

"Agata would be furious if he heard you."

"No kidding," replied Wein with a laugh. "Well, I've got a few ideas if we're strapped for cash."

"Like what?"

"Getting it from the filthy rich Roynock and Facrita, for example."

Ninym frowned. She agreed that the prosperous cities would be an excellent source of wealth, but the prince was hardly on great terms with either. How could Wein procure the money?

He already had an answer.

"Why, we'll just do a bit of business."

A knock sounded at the door. It was Agata's aide, Kamil.

"Pardon me, Prince Wein. I've made the purchase using the remaining funds, as you requested."

Ninym tilted her head to one side, unsure what was going on. She noticed a person behind Kamil, and her eyes went wide in recognition.

It was the Flahm slave from the other day.

"Wein, what's going on?!"

He turned to his baffled friend and grinned.

©Falmaro

"Hurry up, Cedric!"

"I'm trying!" the son of a small-time merchant yelled back at his insistent father. The young man was dragging heavy luggage down a road. "Ugh, damn it. Why does this city have so many uphill paths?!"

"Quit your whining. I walked these routes all the time when I was your age. Both ways, too."

"When I'm a big-time merchant, I'm going to buy up all these hills and flatten 'em…!"

"That's the spirit. Careful, your trunk is dragging. Don't drop it for even a second," his father chided.

Cedric quickly adjusted his grip, but he could feel the fatigue in his arms and legs.

"Man, it never ends…!"

As Cedric said, he'd been busier than ever lately. Unlike his days spent killing time in the shop, he now hauled luggage around Muldu and the rest of Ulbeth. The young man would have complained if he were the only one pressed for time, but his father was just as busy and carrying his own pack like Cedric's.

"Quit your griping. This is for your own good, son."

"I know!"

"It's for your own good."

Cedric had heard the phrase often enough, but even he had to admit it was true this time around.

"My wedding is worth the hassle!"

He had a marriage interview. When Cedric heard about it the other day, he thought it was a joke. Even his father had said, *"I don't know what's going on. The news just suddenly came from the higher-ups."* It sounded suspicious.

Further examination confirmed the interview was genuine, leaving Cedric all the more flabbergasted.

The momentous day arrived swiftly. A girl around Cedric's age greeted the trembling, nervous man.

Although the pair were awkward at first, the air began to ring with laughter as the discussion wore on. Cedric met the young woman many more times after that and eventually decided she was the one.

"Now we just have to convince our relatives...!"

When someone in Ulbeth planned to wed, it was customary first to visit the chief members of their family. It was challenging to know what problems might arise later if this step was neglected, and Cedric's round of greetings was the primary reason for his hectic schedule.

"Oh, it's that house over there."

"...You mean the one on that high hill?"

"Exactly. Buck up. If you drop those souvenirs we brought, you'll have to run back home and get more."

"Ghk-ghk-ghk-ghk-ghk...!" Cedric's teeth chattered, and he started to scramble. "Ugh. Damn it, Dad...! Let's get a slave or a porter...!" he complained.

"Don't be pathetic. This is for your marriage, so bear with it."

"That's not what I mean. Like you said, Dad, this is for my own good. I'll do what's necessary. But my new wife's family will probably want to talk business, right? We won't be able to handle everything on our own."

"Ah, I see. I considered that, too, but..."

"Is there a problem?"

A strange look crossed his father's face.

"They've been bought up."

"There are no more slaves to purchase?" Oleom asked upon hearing his subordinate's report.

"Yes. Muldu's acquired them all, apparently," the man confirmed.

Oleom grimaced. Typically, he masked his emotions before his inferiors, but he presently lacked the concentration necessary for that. The reason was, of course, the eastern city. And more specifically, Wein.

That slew of weddings was annoying enough…!

Wein's marriage campaign was a massive thorn in Roynock's side.

In most cases, superiors naturally came to the aid of subordinates looking for a partner. However, Ulbeth's upper crust was lacking candidates. There was no question the fringes of society were being treated as an afterthought.

Wein had targeted this point. Oleom realized the marriage campaign was merely a pretext, and the prince was slowly splitting the opposition from the edges. The West Representative's best option of stopping him was to create weddings of his own.

Regrettably, Oleom could not act upon this. Ulbeth's shackles were too tight. If he tried to force unions together, he'd only create problems elsewhere.

Yet somehow, Wein had sailed past each obstacle like a feat of magic that could never be replicated. In addition to bolstering Muldu, Natra's prince formed marriages between the southern and the western cities. Oleom's position was more stable than Lejoutte's, and this development had created a frustrating crack in their relationship.

By this point, Oleom's sole other option was to demand each

union require approval regardless of faction. However, this would enrage citizens elated by the long-awaited wedding rush. Instead, Oleom zealously visited each allied family to ask for their cooperation and understanding. He had just finished his rounds and was utterly exhausted.

And now, all the slaves had been bought up.

"What was the purpose?"

"No one knows… Muldu snatched them regardless of race, age, or gender."

Oleom had initially assumed Wein would use the slaves for manual labor. He heard Muldu was assembling as many people as possible for their marriage campaign and wondered if the slaves played a role. He quickly discounted this idea, though. Simple manual labor was one thing, but Oleom doubted Wein would entrust a job that required a certain degree of quick thinking and finesse to his new slaves.

Is he planning a large-scale operation? But why this timing…?

These questions tormented the representative, but the answer came soon enough.

"Master Oleom!" a subordinate exclaimed as he flew into the room. "Strange rumors are spreading through town! There's talk of Roynock and Facrita planning simultaneous revolts!"

"What?!" Oleom jolted at this bolt from the blue. "That's ridiculous! Where did you hear that?!"

"I apologize. We're investigating now, but there are still no leads on its origin…! However, the rumors spread across a wide area around the Masquerade!"

"…!" Oleom immediately gritted his teeth.

The Masquerade was a peculiar aspect of Ulbeth culture. It was a gathering where townspeople could wear masks and voice their daily woes under the condition of anonymity.

Oleom felt a cold premonition wash over him as he furiously ruminated on this sudden scenario—there was no mistaking it.

This is also the east's doing!

The Masquerade was always a breeding ground for dissent, but they had targeted this weakness spectacularly.

This barrage of weddings wasn't Agata's style; Wein had to be the mastermind. And even if these new rumors were false, they had spread too far and fast to extinguish.

Still, simultaneous revolts? Is he planning to incite the citizens and take control through military force while I'm focused on his marriage campaign? I admit the people are frustrated, but there's no way they'd be incited by such rumors that swiftly. Wait, wasn't there an incident in central Mealtars where thirty thousand locals rose in protest? I don't remember hearing about Wein's involvement in that, though...

It was not Wein who'd motivated the populace of Mealtars but instead his younger sister, Falanya. Oleom didn't know this detail, but he felt confident that Wein may have played a part in it.

In that case...I see now! He's going to use the slaves to spark chaos!

A man like Wein could move thirty thousand people. Touching the mistreated slaves' hearts and getting them to storm the city would be a simple task. Once they grew violent and the city was in turmoil, the prince would rile the citizens into attacking the upper class.

I must stop this...!

Oleom's mind frantically raced.

"...Are there any slaves left at the market?" he asked.

"Yes, a few, I believe."

"Buy them all up. Don't let Muldu take any more. And send someone to Altie immediately."

"Altie?"

Oleom nodded. "We need weapons. Buy the north city's entire stock and any farming equipment that can be used as armaments."

Wein couldn't start a revolt without equipment. He'd need it if he hoped to gather the slaves and citizens under his banner, and Altie had the greatest supply in all of the Alliance.

It'll be reassuring to have a stockpile of weapons in the unlikely event I need to raise my own force! I can get ahead of the curve and control the arms race! Oleom girded his resolve.

Don't underestimate me, Wein Salema Arbalest. Ulbeth won't be your plaything!

"—C'mon, try harder than that. It's like you guys *want* me to eat you up."

Wein frowned, a sheet of paper in one hand. It was a contract with a merchant from Altie. The terms stated the current surplus of weapons, plus all made in the next six months, would be sold to Muldu. In addition, the arms included in this deal would soon make their way to Roynock and Facrita. Wein sold them for triple the price.

"After buying up all the weapons in secret, you purchased all the slaves, spread rumors of a revolt, and sowed panic in the western and the southern cities. Then, when they wanted armaments, you sold them to each side for triple the price... You really are crooked."

Ninym stared at the prince with exasperation. Still, there was no other way to get money from Roynock and Facrita. Wein had earned the funds by producing nonexistent fear. "Incidentally, were you really planning to start a revolt?"

"Nope," Wein replied plainly. "Couldn't do it if I tried. Falanya moved the people of Mealtars, and they had turned to her out of desperation. That's not easy to replicate."

In short, it was a bluff. The ruling classes of Roynock and Facrita didn't know that, however, and played right into the palm of his hand.

"Anyway, our wallet is nice and fat again. Now the marriage campaign can move full steam ahead."

Wein nodded to himself with satisfaction. His attitude suggested the matter was settled, but Ninym hesitantly called out from beside him.

"...Hey, Wein." He looked over at her. She felt his gaze and continued. "Did you really need to buy the slaves?"

"We've got the money now, right? Besides, they can help us gather info in Ulbeth, then come to Natra. Or stay with Agata. Whatever they want, really."

"That's not what I mean…"

Wein had purchased almost one hundred people. A dozen or so were Flahm, including the man Ninym had met.

"Um…I was just wondering…if maybe…"

"'It's fine.'" Wein grinned. "Isn't that what you said?"

"…"

Wein had noticed her strange behavior that day and the reason for it. He must have figured everything out and…

"…Thank you."

"Why, whatever for?" Wein asked with an innocent shrug.

Ninym smiled softly.

"Let's prepare our next move. Oleom and Lejoutte won't sit still for long," Wein stated, changing the topic.

The Flahm girl nodded.

©Falmaro

"Yes, I doubt they'll stand for this. Do you think Roynock and Facrita will join forces?"

"Both cities are in chaos after being blindsided, but their leaders can handle it. The duo will try and team up again once they've reassured everyone. Unfortunately…" Wein grinned. "I'm here to stop 'em."

"You're up to no good again."

"If I was *really* up to no good, there'd be nothing left."

"That's…entirely accurate."

"You were supposed to disagree, Miss Ninym!"

Ninym ignored the gripe. "So what exactly do you have in mind?"

"It's simple," the prince said with another smirk. "I'll use their fractured strength to my advantage."

It was the dead of night.

A single figure traversed the moonlit backstreets of a particular city. A hood concealed their eyes as they soundlessly continued through the alley until finally arriving at a small house. The shadow knocked three times. No answer. They entered regardless.

"…"

The interior was dim and sparsely furnished. A masked man occupied a chair that had been placed next to a simple desk.

"I'm sorry I took so long," the shadow greeted, pulling back their hood.

The seated man likewise removed his mask to reveal, of all people, West Representative Oleom. "Ah, Lejoutte. I'm glad you made it."

Yes, the cowled figure's identity was indeed Lejoutte.

They were alone, and neither had told anyone their destination. Thus, this could only be a secret rendezvous between the two representatives.

"My dear Oleom!" Lejoutte took off her mask and flew straight into Oleom's arms.

"I panicked when I heard those alarming rumors. I'm so glad you're safe."

"I was worried, too, Lejoutte. Seeing you here shines a light on my troubled heart."

The two smiled in one another's embrace. Although Roynock and Facrita were currently allies, each side had secret ambitions to outwit the other. Yet their representatives were undeniably lovers.

"We were so close to fulfilling our dream, yet look at us now," Lejoutte remarked, her expression twisted by frustration.

Oleom cupped her cheek and nodded. "Rallying the western and the southern cities, becoming allies, and uniting as both representatives and symbols of peace... It was all coming together."

Yes, this was the truth no one else knew.

Before rising to power, Oleom and Lejoutte were two young people in love. However, each was a family member of their respective city's representative. Announcing their relationship without due consideration would cause backlash and make life a living hell.

Neither could cast aside the feelings burning within them, however, so the pair chose to fight back.

First, Oleom and Lejoutte rose to power by intentionally adopting foreign knowledge to surpass the flood of other candidates.

Next, they pretended to be political rivals while bolstering the economic relationship between their cities and demonstrating the partnership's advantages. Roynock and Facrita had slowly grown close to the point where it would require only a little nudging to finalize the bond. Then Oleom and Lejoutte could be married at last.

If the couple couldn't be together for love, they'd gladly use politics and profit to justify it. That was their grand scheme for eternal romance. Unfortunately, a devil had interfered. The visitor from Natra, Wein Salema Arbalest.

"Dear Oleom, how is Roynock faring?"

"The marriage campaign and whispers of revolt have riled the citizens. I'm trying to calm them, but the results are mixed... What about you?"

"I'm having similar trouble. Animosity toward the Muldu and Roynock is growing each day. I'm doing my best to defend your name, but..."

"I've heard the tales, but Prince Wein really isn't someone you want for an enemy," Oleom groaned.

"Should we mobilize our forces?" Lejoutte asked soberly.

If the western and the southern cities joined forces, their combined military had a good chance of overpowering Muldu. For all his strategic ability, Wein would be helpless against an army.

However, Oleom rejected this proposal.

"No, that isn't wise. Agata is a Holy Elite, and Prince Wein is a foreign leader. If we attack them without just cause, it will greatly hinder future governance of the Alliance."

Had Oleom and Lejoutte never studied the world beyond their borders, they may have employed a military approach. The pair understood that Ulbeth was the "backwoods of the West," however, and knew that armed assault was ill-advised. Agata could be defeated only through lawful channels, and Wein would need to be sent home to Natra in one piece.

"It's all right. Our skills will lead us to success. The Signing

Ceremony is coming up. If we can unseat Agata there, Prince Wein will have to return to Natra."

"So the ceremony is our best chance to take control of our factions?"

Oleom nodded. "But Prince Wein may resort to violence even if we don't. Be careful, Lejoutte."

"I understand. Please take care as well, dear Oleom."

"I swear I won't die until the day I can embrace you in front of the whole world."

Oleom and Lejoutte held hands.

"Our situation feels tense right now, but it's a minor nuisance compared to what *that other couple* went through. Let's fight together."

"Yes, Oleom."

Together, they would surpass any obstacle. Oleom and Lejoutte kissed, conviction burning in their hearts.

But those feelings were soon betrayed.

"...What did you just say?"

Several days after his rendezvous with Lejoutte, Oleom sharply questioned his subordinate's latest report.

"Ah, well, you see..." Overwhelmed though he was by his superior's aura, the man repeated his message. "Rumors are spreading through the city that you and the South Representative are romantically involved..."

"...!"

Rage showed plainly on Oleom's face, but it was only an act he put on in front of his servant. Internally, he was dumbfounded.

How were we discovered…?!

His secret meetings with Lejoutte were always at a different time and location, and he took meticulous precautions. They couldn't have been caught so easily.

Still, gossip was spreading. There was no denying that the truth had leaked.

Is this another one of Wein's tricks?! Was he eyeing our movements?!

Wein and his delegation didn't know the lay of the land, and Agata's forces were no doubt focused on the marriage campaign. Did he really have spare resources? Or was he putting his slaves to work?

No…I bet he didn't even check if it was true!

Everyone knew there was a marriage boom in the Ulbeth Alliance. It was also common knowledge Oleom and Lejoutte were concerned these weddings would enfeeble their factions and hoped to curtail them.

Now rumors were spreading of a love affair between the two representatives. While they decried marriage among the populace, they were engaging in secret meetings. Moreover, Oleom and Lejoutte acted as bitter enemies in public. This was sufficient fodder even without solid evidence.

…At any rate, I need a counterattack!

It wasn't like Oleom could ignore this fragmented truth. Not to mention the mess he'd have to deal with if Wein found substantial evidence. Oleom had to dampen the rumors, and quickly.

"I won't allow such disrespectful lies. Find the source and apprehend the criminal. Catch the irresponsible gossipers spreading the falsehoods, too."

"Understood…" The subordinate nodded, then nervously added, "Master Oleom…there is one more issue."

"There's more?"

Oleom's eyes shot open at what he heard next.

"There's a motion to impeach me…?!" Lejoutte stood from her seat when she heard the news. "What's the meaning of this?! Why propose such a thing?!"

"In response to your marriage policies and the rumor of your affair with the West Representative, Master Huanshe and several other leaders held a meeting on the matter."

"Ngh…! Now is not the time for that!" Lejoutte shouted angrily. She realized the futility of this outburst and shook her head. "I'm sorry. Taking my frustration out on you won't solve anything."

"Think nothing of it. But, Lady Lejoutte, if things continue as they are…"

The woman's servant trailed off, but the implication was plain. This situation wasn't ideal, and Oleom was undoubtedly in the same boat.

Representatives had to come from their city's designated family. Altie had lost their family, so there was no one to fill the position, but Roynock and Facrita still had theirs. If Oleom and Lejoutte fell, other relatives would take their places.

Conversely, contenders who hoped to become representatives themselves saw the pair as a nuisance. For instance, many were aware that the man mentioned earlier, Huanshe, had long sought the role. Even if Lejoutte thought this was no time to be discussing impeachment, Huanshe could ask for no more excellent opportunity.

"A few proposing impeachment are also insisting that you be immediately taken into custody and a new representative chosen."

"Honestly, they're incorrigible...but sitting here twiddling our thumbs won't help."

If anything, the situation had been steadily deteriorating since Wein's arrival. Lejoutte couldn't believe she now had to fight her own faction on top of her foe in Muldu.

"I'll hold a meeting soon. Make the necessary preparations."

"Yes."

As she issued orders, Lejoutte's thoughts drifted to Oleom, who was undoubtedly suffering through an identical predicament.

Please be safe, Oleom... Lejoutte prayed silently to herself.

"I suppose you could say it's factional pride," Wein said as he read over reports about the western and the southern cities. "If Muldu were stronger, the factions would likely still be operating smoothly. However, any standard attack is enough to topple this city. Total victory."

"And that's what allowed infighting this late in the game."

Wein nodded.

Oleom and Lejoutte already had their hands full with Muldu but now had to deal with growing dissatisfaction and dubious scandals as well. For anyone hoping to drag them through the mud, it was a perfect opportunity.

The two representatives could warn the allies that were hoping to unseat them of the lurking threat, but how much good would it do? Those eager to snatch power from Oleom and Lejoutte wouldn't sense the same danger.

"Man, the western and the southern cities sure have it rough."

"It's strange to watch someone use their piece's own weakness to manipulate a foe."

"It's nothing special. Weakness and strength are just strategies. Strength can give you an easy victory, but even weakness can take down a king if you know how to use it. The key is method and timing."

A knock came at the door, and Kamil walked in.

"Prince Wein, I have new information on Roynock and Facrita, but…"

"Oleom and Lejoutte are busy keeping all their ducks in a row, right?"

Wein's tone was confident, but Kamil was nervous as he answered.

"About that…"

"What? What happened?" Wein asked, the questions tumbling out of his mouth.

Kamil steeled himself.

"…It seems the pair have eloped."

Wein and Ninym looked at each other.

"All right, do you need anything else?"

Ninym stood in a deserted mansion on the outskirts of Muldu.

"No, we're very comfortable, thanks to you," a man replied. He was the same Flahm slave she'd met the other day. Wein had recently purchased him. "Words cannot express our gratitude. You've both rescued us from servitude and allowed us to live as ordinary people."

Wein had strategically bought up every slave in Ulbeth and now had to see to the task of feeding and clothing them all. Their accommodations also needed to be spacious enough to house the large group of previously scattered people. Wein used Kamil's connections to rent an empty mansion in the suburbs and prepare it for immediate occupancy.

"I'm glad to hear it. I will inform Prince Wein."

"Thank you very much."

The slaves were ethnically diverse, but since Ninym was their primary go-between, the Flahm slave became the group's representative as a matter of course. Fortunately, he seemed to have a degree of sophistication and skillfully managed the role.

"Has everyone decided upon their future plans as I requested earlier?"

"The majority wish to migrate to Natra. However, quite a few are still undecided."

Although the enslaved people officially belonged to Wein, his attitude was very hands-off. They were free to go wherever they wished, or they could help him out in Ulbeth and emigrate to Natra afterward.

"Understood. Prince Wein will be in Ulbeth awhile yet, so ask them to consider in the meantime. We can't wait forever, but there's still room for compromise."

"Yes…" The man nodded before hesitantly adding, "Might I speak on behalf of those who are undecided?"

"Of course. Is something the matter?"

"No, not at all. However, the others and I…feel lost."

"Lost?"

Again, the Flahm man nodded. "Being slaves, we possess no outstanding qualities. Our life's only purpose was to obey our masters and work until we die. Yet we've suddenly been told those days are over."

"…"

"We're grateful, of course. But we don't know why we've been blessed by this unexpected fortune or if we even have the right to accept it. We cannot hope to repay such kindness…"

I see, Ninym thought. She understood where he was coming from. Their surprise windfall and sudden new circumstances left them feeling ungrounded. It gave Ninym pause to reveal the actual reason Wein had bought them. The young woman took a moment to find the right words.

"…You needn't worry over that. Prince Wein is a man of great benevolence who often reaches out to the unfortunate. If you wish to repay his generosity, he would love nothing more than for you to live well as citizens of Natra. Of course, you may also go elsewhere. You are free."

It was a shallow statement, and the Flahm man didn't appear

particularly moved. However, there was nothing more Ninym could say. Nothing except—

"If you are still uneasy, Prince Wein is looking to fill positions. He requires workers and people who know the land, so you may consider those if you wi—"

"Of course!" the man answered before Ninym could finish her sentence. "Ah, forgive me. Everyone would appreciate the opportunity. For we who have nothing, it will bring us great comfort to proudly serve His Highness."

"In that case, I hope you are ready. I have the details here, but I'd like to give a verbal explanation as well. Can you call everyone to the reception room?"

"Yes, right away."

The man turned on his heel to leave the room, but Ninym called out behind him.

"Just a moment. There's something I'd like to ask you."

"Yes, what is it?" the man asked, looking back at her with a tilt of his head.

Ninym closed her eyes.

"…Why did you smile that day?"

"So, the reps eloped. Didn't see that one coming," Wein remarked with a sigh back in Agata's estate.

Kamil, Agata's aide, stood beside him instead of Ninym.

"I understand we spread rumors about a romantic affair, but did you already know of their relationship, Prince?"

"Not at all. I just tossed the story out there whether it was true or not."

In this era, hard evidence was difficult to come by, so what mattered most was the authority, wealth, and reputation of the accused, as well as their opponent's lack thereof. Wein's strategy dealt a heavy blow to Oleom and Lejoutte's prestige, and there had already been others hoping to drag the pair down. These combined factors made even baseless accusations of a relationship as believable as cold, hard facts.

"So those lies turned out to be true, and now the representatives have eloped. It's a shocking turn of events," Kamil remarked.

Wein's reply was quiet and doubtful. "I'm not sure that's the case."

"...What do you mean?"

"Oleom and Lejoutte wouldn't outright announce they were eloping. That's just what some Roynock and Facrita officials claimed. Isn't there a good chance something else is going on?"

"The two apparently left a note behind."

"That's easy enough to forge. Their story has as much evidence as the rumors I started."

Kamil groaned softly and sank into thought for a moment. After a bit, he posed a question.

"More than a few people would certainly benefit from their disappearance. But if you're correct, why would the representatives' adversaries choose elopement? They could have reported their vanishing as some kind of accident."

Wein already had an answer.

"In a touch-and-go situation like this, any conspicuous 'accident' would look unnatural. Those eager for Oleom and Lejoutte's positions would become the targets of suspicion, and their authority would be undermined from the outset. It's the same as hurting your own crown by violently usurping the throne. Not a helpful solution in the long run."

"In that case, couldn't they fake a double suicide? Two rumored lovers taking their own lives before fate can separate them sounds quite plausible."

"An act like that would make them martyrs to the masses." Wein adopted a dramatic tone as he went on. " '*Society has separated the star-crossed lovers! Oh, how tragic that they could be together only in death! Whoever would drive them to such a fate?!*' Can't you hear it already?"

"…Yes, I see what you mean. However, even if the opposition did announce a lovers' suicide, I'm certain you would generate that very scenario, Prince," Kamil replied with both awe and dread.

Wein did not comment, and Kamil took this silence as affirmation.

"At any rate, I understand now why the southern and the western cities chose elopement. 'The representatives disappeared from the political stage because they fell to the temptations of love.' Yes, that would receive the least protest."

"Of course, there's always the chance they *did* run away together. I'd say it's a fifty-fifty shot. If the announcement is a lie and the competition actually caught the two, their chances of survival are around seventy percent."

"I'm surprised. You're that certain they'll keep them alive?"

"The situation is still chaotic. Oleom and Lejoutte are useful scapegoats, and once they lose all support, the captors can step forward and earn credibility by forcing the ousted pair to declare a transfer of power. Still, it wouldn't surprise me if they were killed before they could become a nuisance."

"…" Kamil went silent.

"Something wrong?"

"Ah, no, forgive me. So the West and the South Representatives' absence will give us an advantage," Kamil stated as he returned to himself.

Wein nodded. "Right. A surprise transition won't be easy, and we can strike hard while everyone else is occupied."

Wein remained focused on splitting the opposition, and his plans were coming along well. At this rate, Muldu would regain enough authority to give Roynock and Facrita a run for their money, if not surpass them.

"The western and the southern cities will set aside their differences if we push too hard, so it's a fine line. We'll discuss the particulars with Ninym later."

"Come to think of it, where is Lady Ninym?"

"She's with the slaves. Can't just leave them hanging, after all."

Kamil's following words were weighty. "I understand such a force has put pressure on Roynock and Facrita, but to even allow them a mansion…"

"Something wrong with that?"

"No, I'm just deeply impressed. I've heard the Flahm live in Natra without fear of persecution. Although merciless to your enemies, you truly are a kind man, Prince Wein."

Kamil's comment was heartfelt, but…

"'Kind,' huh?" Wein smirked faintly. "Come to think of it, my sister said the same thing before I left—"

The balcony looked over a silvery landscape. The northernmost nation of Natra was already blanketed in snow.

Could her brother in the Ulbeth Alliance enjoy the same

scene? Did an unfamiliar country and city share the same winter wonderland?

As Falanya pondered this absentmindedly, someone draped a jacket over her shoulders.

"...Nanaki."

The princess turned to find that Nanaki had appeared by her side at some point. The young man with pure white hair and fiery red eyes stared at Falanya.

"Put your arms through the sleeves. It's cold out here."

Falanya obeyed and wore the jacket properly. She hadn't realized how cold she was until she donned the coat, and a faint warmth filled her. However, even the extra heat didn't ease her tensed expression. She continued to gaze at the winter scene solemnly. Nanaki faced her and spoke again.

"Has the shock not worn off yet?"

"Huh?"

Falanya looked up at Nanaki, and he pressed on.

"Wein told you, right? About the Flahm's history."

"..."

Falanya stared into Nanaki's eyes. The boy rarely showed emotion, yet it wasn't as though he'd never known anger, happiness, or sadness. Even now, his profile was blank—or so most people would've thought.

Falanya saw it differently, however. She could see the subtle shift in Nanaki's features. At present, he seemed rather downcast.

She also could guess the reason.

"Yes, you're right. I was shocked to learn of the massacres the Flahm committed."

The Flahm man known as the "Founder" elected to create his

©Falmaro

own deity after a journey to find gods proved none existed. The result was the one true God.

Wein said the Founder must have felt this was a divine revelation. Most deities needed something to rule. A forest god held dominion over a forest, a river god over a river, and a mountain god over a mountain. This made them easier to visualize and believe in.

Yet those divine beings who dwelt within such things also lost influence when their territory was destroyed. On his travels, the Founder realized humans would inevitably cut down the forests, dam the rivers, carve the mountains, and destroy the objects of their worship.

He required an eternal, sacred land far from mankind's reach. How ironic that the divine guardians of humanity needed protection from their own devotees.

And so the Founder embarked on another quest.

The oceans were no good. People would conquer the seas someday. The sky wouldn't work either, as humans would come to rule them, too. Even the stars were dubious. Humanity would touch them eventually.

Where, then? Where could his Flahm brethren worship their God without fear of loss? No modern-day instrument could measure the Founder's mental agony.

Then a revolutionary idea finally struck him. He could *create* an untouchable land for his invented monotheism, the one and only ruler of all creation.

"This True God spread among the Flahm. Connected by a shared belief, the people began uniting to protect themselves…" Nanaki explained.

Let's create our own country. A Flahm nation where we can live freely.

Such a wish was only natural. The Flahm worshiped God, fell under its creator's banner, and used what little funds and knowledge they had to get started.

Many records in Natra revealed that this was not a painless process. Nonetheless, the Flahm overcame all obstacles to form history's first Flahm Kingdom.

"But after that…"

The omens of destruction were present from the very first dynasty.

Erecting the nation's framework required more hands than the Flahm could provide on their own. So they had to incorporate other races.

The Flahm's fate probably would have been much different if they could forget the past and come together with other cultures. However, their pain and hatred had festered. As the new overlords, the Flahm exacted revenge like it was their birthright. Massacre and tyranny reigned.

"…Did Wein tell you what the Flahm used to call themselves?" Nanaki inquired. Falanya shook her head. Nanaki played with the ends of his hair as he went on. "Angels."

"Angels…?"

"The One True God's backstory had a plot hole. If he ruled over everything, why did he only protect the Flahm?"

A Flahm man had created the religion, so it was hardly surprising. Still, the Founder hated even the slightest flaw and thus thought up a reason.

"The Founder targeted our primary source of oppression, our eyes and hair. He claimed the Flahm were not human, but angels sent from heaven. As divine messengers, we were superior to mortals. Our unique features were proof of that."

The Flahm's white hair and crimson eyes could possess an ethereal quality depending on the viewer's perspective. These characteristics attracted attention and persecution, but the Founder turned this on its head. He proposed the Flahm didn't just look otherworldly—they *were*.

"The Flahm were oppressed for so long that they had become trapped in a slave mentality. The Founder claimed they were angels to wipe that away."

While unusual, the plan ultimately succeeded. The physical attributes the Flahm once detested became blessings from God, and they felt a new rush of pride as his messengers.

However, the Founder could never have anticipated what would follow.

How would the Flahm, who believed they were angels, treat those who had wronged them now that they had the upper hand?

"Wein said they responded in kind."

"He was being nice. I heard it was horrible."

Records of the Flahm's horrific, indescribable atrocities existed in various places across the West. They spoke of a cold-blooded people who threw countless lives into the depths of despair.

A nation built on blood and deep resentment was doomed to fail. The Flahm rule quickly fell, and its people were cast into slavery once more. No, their position was even worse.

The oppressed Flahm, who had once raised a flag of revolution, became the very sort they fought against.

As a side note, a particular insurgency leader targeted the Flahm's religion. He added details to the Flahm's fictitious monotheism to suit their purposes and strove to make it Varno's primary deity.

The man who went on to establish the continent's greatest religion was Levetia.

"—But that was a long time ago, Falanya. You can't change the past," Nanaki said. "Or do you fear the Flahm of today?"

He posed this question with resolute eyes. Nanaki's people had murdered thousands. If his master admitted she was afraid of him, he'd vow never to show his face again.

"No, not at all."

Falanya took Nanaki's hands as if embracing his determination. Had he grown? His palms and fingers used to match hers, yet they felt larger now.

"It's true that I was shocked at first. But like you said, it's ancient history. I care more about this jacket you put around me than what others did long ago."

"...I see." Nanaki gave a slight nod, and Falanya noticed the relief in his subtle words and gestures. "But then, why were you staring off?"

Nanaki initially thought Falanya was still in shock, but if he understood correctly, she had already processed her feelings about Flahm's dark past.

"...I told Wein that, like many kings before him, he's a gentle person who treats the Flahm well and gives them a home in Natra. At least here they can live in peace."

Falanya recalled how Wein had lightly smiled at her praise before responding with a question.

"Falanya, do I really seem kind to the Flahm?"

She couldn't answer right away. Wein had appointed Ninym and the other Flahm to responsible positions. His actions since becoming regent left no reason to doubt his generosity.

As a politician, he obviously had to make tough decisions sometimes. If Falanya had still been the sheltered princess who only knew life in the palace and believed her brother was kind to the core, she would have nodded immediately.

"But I couldn't."

Although inexperienced, Falanya had visited various nations as part of the Natra delegation. Something in Wein's question had kept her from answering right away.

"Wein is nice to the Flahm... No, to everyone. But..."

What had he been trying to tell her? And why couldn't she give a clear "yes"? Falanya had been pondering this all alone.

"Then you should investigate," Nanaki suggested.

"Investigate...?"

"Whether or not Wein is kind. I don't think so, but I'm not saying I'm right. You wouldn't believe me anyway. You'll just have to look into it and decide for yourself."

"That's—"

Nanaki's thoughts on the prince weren't the least bit surprising. If anything, they reminded Falanya of something.

That's right... Wein said people are multifaceted.

People act differently depending on the place and the situation. Each side is just a fraction of their personality.

And so a thought struck Falanya. Wein was her ideal brother, but what if she was only noticing the qualities that made him that way?

In that case, the purpose of his inquiry was...

Wein had probably realized his sister was observing only one side of him and had pointed this out as a question. To tell Falanya he was more than kind—to broaden her perspective.

"You're right, Nanaki," Falanya replied, suddenly looking up. "If I don't know how Wein really feels about the people, I should find out."

Nanaki's tone was tinged with relief. "It looks like you're feeling better."

"Yes. And that being the case, we should get started right away. First...I should talk to Sirgis. Wein told him to help me."

As Falanya's mind swirled with ideas, and as Nanaki watched, he thought, *Even without my help, Falanya would have made this decision on her own.*

Once the princess realized Wein was attempting to teach a life lesson, there'd be no stopping her. And even if Falanya missed his intentions, she would have eventually questioned her brother's true nature.

The real mystery is why Wein used himself as an example.

If he wanted to give Falanya a bigger perspective, he could have used something more innocuous. What was the purpose of citing himself?

Nanaki didn't think Wein was kind. What advantage would he gain if Falanya reached the same conclusion and grew disillusioned?

Was it unintentional? Perhaps he was confident she wouldn't be disappointed? Or...

Maybe he *wanted* to disappoint her?

It's useless. I have no clue what that guy is thinking.

Nanaki brushed off these strange thoughts and focused on his duty. He was Falanya's guard. Avoiding distractions and keeping her safe was enough.

Yes, he'd protect her from *any* foe.

After speaking with the slaves' representative, Ninym headed down an alley on her way back to Wein's Muldu mansion. It was dusk, and not many were milling around. It was perfect for someone like Ninym, who wished to avoid attention. On this particular occasion, she was too preoccupied to notice, however.

Why?

Ninym's mind was elsewhere as she kept to the side of the road.

Why can't I just let it go?

She recalled her question to the Flahm man and still wondered what she'd been thinking. He wouldn't have brought up the incident on his own, but Ninym had asked anyway. The man was in no position to refuse her. He'd adopted a troubled expression and took a moment to select his words carefully.

"I wanted to comfort a Flahm child on the verge of tears."

His answer pierced Ninym like a sword.

Between the two of them, she was clearly better off. Yet rather than beg for help or vent his jealousy and resentment, he'd consoled a child of his kin. And all the while, she'd been pondering about how to abandon him!

If this were the old dynasty...

The oppressed-turned-oppressors. If modern Flahm shared the same mindset, they'd be cut down in an instant. Ninym thought that was likely for the best.

However, most living Flahm were good, simple people. And although Ninym kept her duty to Natra's royal family above all else, her Flahm heart still wavered.

Brethren, family, unity...

Ninym Ralei's blood was intertwined with history, whether she liked it or not. It had been a source of frustration on more than one occasion. If only she could be free of those shackles and serve Wein simply as herself.

No such wish would save her, though.

I'm sure I would have tried something on my own if Wein hadn't eased my anxiety.

Ninym labeled herself a failure, a weakling. As she trudged along with a heavy heart...

"Ah, Lady Ninym." The young woman heard her name and looked up to see Kamil standing before her. "Are you returning to the mansion?"

Ninym cleared her mind and nodded. "Yes. What about you, Sir Kamil?"

"I am on my way to devise our next steps."

"Ah, I see…"

Most of Agata's subordinates were busy carrying out Wein's plans. Even Kamil, who was usually by Agata's side, had to run around Ulbeth. The prince would have liked to send out his own people, but they weren't much help in an unfamiliar land. Although the Natra delegation assisted with odd jobs, Agata's servants handled the heavy lifting.

"Please let me know if there is anything I can do."

"Thank you, but I'll be speaking with Altie. I'm afraid they don't take foreigners very seriously."

"Is the northern city really that insular?"

"It's always been a place of small-minded craftsmen, but I heard the loss of their representative family exacerbated their prejudice. The people of Altie themselves chose to execute them, though, so they got what they deserved."

Got what they deserved.

Kamil's tone was oddly cold. Perhaps self-aware, he shook his head lightly to collect himself and flashed a smile.

"But I digress. There's no need to worry. Fatigue is rewarding, so long as I know that the end results benefit Master Agata," he said. "Are you all right, Lady Ninym? You seem to be staggering."

"I dare not say I'm tired to someone so busy, Sir Kamil."

"Oh dear. It seems I've been bested," the young man replied with a frown.

"I'm joking," Ninym clarified. "I'm just overwhelmed by the new environment. I'll report to His Highness and go to bed early tonight."

Kamil nodded. "Yes, a fine idea. Well then, please excuse me. It will be dark soon, so take care on your way back, Lady Ninym."

"Yes, thank you. I will."

Ninym watched the attendant leave, then resumed her own walk. She was feeling a bit better. Maybe talking with Kamil helped.

I need to stop thinking about myself all the time.

Like she told Kamil, she would report to Wein and then head to sleep.

Suddenly, Ninym's thoughts came to an abrupt halt.

"..."

Her eyes narrowed as adrenaline raced through her body. The Flahm woman took a breath and dashed into the nearest backstreet. The sun was setting, and the path was already pitch black. Still, Ninym didn't stop.

There were voices behind her. Ninym sensed multiple pursuers, yet she remained calm. After all, they sprang into action *because* she'd noticed them.

I'm still pretty far from the mansion...!

The slaves were set up in a manor on the city's outskirts—Agata's territory. Muldu was already short on hands, and Ninym had carelessly gone alone because she'd thought it would be a quick trip.

Should she try to escape or ask someone nearby for help? Ninym considered these possibilities but stopped before choosing either.

A masked man was barring the way forward in the alley.

"You must be Prince Wein's servant." His voice was flat as he stared at her from behind his mask. "We'd like you to come with us."

"..."

Ninym could sense this man was skilled. She'd probably win in a one-on-one fight, but it would take time. Those pursuing her from behind were undoubtedly his cohorts. Fending off multiple enemies was a tall order.

Calling for help won't do much good if these people know I'm a Flahm. They could claim I'm an escaped slave...

In that case, she had one option, to win this fight before backup arrived.

Sensing Ninym's intent, the man made the first move.

"Do not resist. You might regret it."

"Is that a threat?"

"No. I've been instructed to treat you with utmost courtesy," the man replied. "Instead, I'll burn that house filled with slaves to the ground."

"—!"

Ninym couldn't hide her horror. It was horrifying that the slaves were being used as hostages, but it was surprising that the man saw their value as captives in the first place.

New slaves and a royal aide. Most would never imagine the two went together. Using them as a bargaining tool against Ninym indicated he was aware of her complex feelings.

Naturally, the young woman kept such emotions concealed, but her conduct and attitude might have exposed things. It was a troubling notion to realize that the man's informant was someone who'd observed her closely enough to learn her secrets.

"If you have orders, then you work for a superior. Who is it?"

"I am not at liberty to say."

Questioning him was futile, and Ninym's pursuers had caught up in the intervening time. There was nowhere to run.

Ninym scowled as she squeezed out her following words. "…Fine. Take me wherever you want."

The sun had already set by the time the men and Ninym disappeared down the dark street.

"Our plan appears to be proceeding smoothly," Agata remarked calmly in his office.

"Yeah, we couldn't have done it without your help," Wein replied. This was a joint scheme, so the two had regular meetings. "At this rate, our chances of tipping the scales by the Signing Ceremony are lookin' pretty good. Isn't it *great*, Agata? You'll get your unified Ulbeth Alliance after all."

Agata didn't take the bait.

"We can rejoice once we're victorious."

"Are you saying something else is going to happen?"

"We must always expect the unexpected."

"The unexpected, huh…?" Wein repeated teasingly. "Muldu is rising up while Roynock and Facrita are in total chaos. Who's going to make a move? Altie? They can't do anything without a representative. I feel kind of bad for them. They had to execute their whole representative family for collusion, then got cut off at the knee afterward."

"*It wasn't collusion,*" Agata cut in sharply. "The North Representative didn't conspire with anyone."

"Oh…? But that's what I heard earlier. The Ulbeth documents I've read say the same thing."

"That was the official reason. However, the truth tells otherwise.

Gerde Croon, the North Representative, was the victim of premeditated murder. And the Altie citizens are the culprits."

Wein's eyes flashed with curiosity. He knew from Agata's manner that this was no joke. Why would the populace decide to kill their protector?

"Around twenty years ago, our techniques plateaued, our culture curdled, and traditions lost all meaning. Rampant supremacism had caused the Ulbeth Alliance to stagnate." Agata paused. "Concerned about the situation, Croon and his wife took action. There was no question they acted with love for their city. The couple sensed that a foreign nation might swallow up Ulbeth if we remained static."

"They saw the writing on the wall, huh? And that's why they reached out to another country?"

"Yes. They visited the Casskard Kingdom, a nation north of Altie. Croon and his wife studied their culture and ideology, hoping it might give the Ulbeth Alliance a second chance. Regrettably..."

The couple's efforts were in vain. Ulbeth's conservative populace considered their representative's reformist views strange, and they ostracized him.

"If word of their deeds had never spread beyond Altie, the couple could have quietly retired. However, news spread to the other cities, and Croon and his wife were soon viewed as traitors. The people of the northern city had to offer up their heads to prove their own innocence."

The entire Croon family was executed for conspiracy.

Consequentially, Altie was exploited by the other cities in the Alliance because they now lacked a representative. Altie's citizens regretted their actions, but it was too late.

"...Let's return to our previous conversation. I have no intention of underestimating anyone. Altie's people are waiting for a long-lost hero to return and a chance for redemption."

"I thought the whole bloodline was eradicated?"

"It was. Yet there are many stories of noble descendants of supposedly long-dead lineages returning to save their fellows."

Altie's populace believed this. They endured each day because they were certain salvation was coming.

"I see. So you're saying the northern city is a ticking time bomb. It's definitely better to play it safe."

Wein had only Agata's word to go on, but he didn't believe the man was lying. Still, there was no telling how much of the tale was trustworthy either. Especially since he was almost positive that Agata was plotting against him.

I should ask Ninym to investigate more when she gets back.

No sooner had the thought crossed the prince's mind than...

"—Excuse me! Is Prince Wein here?!"

Kamil, who should have been in negotiations with Altie, rushed into the room. He was out of breath.

"What's up? Did Altie give you a hard time?"

Looking uncharacteristically flustered, Kamil shook his head. "N-no, everything went well. However, well, please look at this...!"

Kamil handed Wein a single letter. Surprised Kamil would show him first rather than Agata, Wein cocked his head as he read over the missive.

His expression froze.

"Prince Wein?" Agata asked, grim expectation in his voice.

Wein only stared at the letter. He kept reading it, but the contents didn't change. After a prolonged silence, he finally replied, "It seems...Ninym has been captured."

Agata's face darkened, and Kamil looked at Wein sorrowfully.

"They say she will be returned safely if we leave Roynock and Facrita alone… Taking the letter at face value, this could be the work of either city."

"…What will you do?" The significance of Agata's question spoke for itself. Everyone in the room knew Wein's answer here could end things.

The prince sighed heavily.

"We have to concede. I wouldn't call it 'fortunate,' but they're only requesting that we cease further action, not undo what we've already done. There are other ways to raise Muldu's standing. We just have to be flexible."

He wouldn't abandon Ninym, but he'd cooperate with Agata for as long as possible. That was Wein's answer.

"With that in mind, call back your forces, Kamil."

"Ah, well, you see…" Kamil glanced at Agata. The older man gave a slight nod.

"Do as he says. We can't continue the marriage campaign without Prince Wein anyway."

"U-understood… Incidentally, Prince Wein, if further demands are made…"

"I'll kill them before that happens."

Wein's response was flat. There was no question he'd do it.

"Have your men look for Ninym. We'll rethink our strategy once we find her and know she's safe."

"Y-yes!"

Kamil hurried out of the room as quickly as he'd entered.

"…To think they would go to such extremes," Agata muttered once he and the prince were alone again. If his hunch was correct, the Flahm girl was safe. Any kidnapper who recognized her value

©Falmaro

as a hostage would take care to remain civil. If, by some chance, she *wasn't* safe, however…

The fury of this dragon in front of me will burn Ulbeth to the ground.

On the outside, Wein seemed composed as usual. However, Agata had observed many people in his long career and knew the prince's heart was currently a violent swirl of emotions. If Agata had suggested abandoning the aide only moments before, those would have been his final words.

A dragon's imperial wrath had been provoked. It would not be quelled easily.

"Still, this is excellent timing," Agata remarked. He retrieved a piece of paper from his breast pocket and tossed it before Wein.

"…What's this?"

"Something you needed and will need again."

Wein took the note and read it. His expression switched from fury to confusion, and he thought for a moment. Then he asked a single question.

"What's going on, Agata?"

The East Representative understood the vague question perfectly.

"I believe you already know this, but the unification of the Ulbeth Alliance was only a front. I have other plans in mind."

"And that's why you're giving me this?"

"Yes. The ceremony is already upon us, so it's fine," Agata continued. "In exchange, I'd like you to hear out my small request once everything is over."

"…"

The two glared at each other for ten seconds or so. Finally Wein answered, "I'll make sure you spill everything."

"It's a promise." Agata dipped his chin and smiled.

Objectively, Ninym was treated with great civility. After leaving with the men, she was led to a carriage, blindfolded, and taken to a mansion in the middle of nowhere.

Although the Flahm woman was locked in a guarded, windowless chamber, it was spacious and well furnished. Ninym could enjoy hot baths and food at her leisure. The place was actually quite comfortable.

Is this a leader's vacation villa?

Ninym wondered if that very leader had staged this abduction, but Ulbeth was a foreign country. She didn't have enough information to guess her captor's identity.

I'd like to escape at least long enough to get a sense of where I am, but...

Fleeing the mansion only to get caught again to map out the surrounding area was a comical notion. Nonetheless, for someone all alone in an unfamiliar place, it wasn't a futile effort.

I wonder how Wein is doing...

Was he okay? Was he worried? How was the enemy using her abduction against him? Ninym was alive, which meant that she still had value as a hostage and that Wein had accepted her captor's demands.

Given the situation, the culprits must be from the western or the southern cities.

Undoubtedly, they were requesting that Wein betray Agata. The prince wasn't the type to meekly concede, however. He'd look for the route to the greatest profit.

Wein is out there doing his best. I have to escape somehow.

Ninym was determined, but security was tight, and there was no chance for her to investigate her surroundings. Just as she was wondering what to do, a knock came at the door.

"Pardon me, Lady Ninym."

A female servant assigned to Ninym entered the room. Her tone was formal, and she gave off the air of one who diligently went about her work. Ninym would have invited her to join Natra's palace staff in any other circumstance.

"What is it? It's too early for a meal."

The servant responded with a polite bow. "My master has returned. He wishes to meet you, Lady Ninym."

"...!"

Master.

Several days had passed since Ninym was taken to the mansion, and she hadn't seen him once. Based on her interactions with her captors and this female servant, he was a capable person with talented and loyal staff. There was no better opportunity to learn more about what was transpiring.

"I'll go now. Lead the way."

The servant led the Flahm woman out of the room with two guards following directly behind. They didn't want to give her a single chance to run off, but such concerns were unwarranted. Ninym had no intention of leaving until she met their master. Nonetheless, she did her best to memorize the building's layout.

"Here we are."

They at last reached their destination, and the servant knocked on the door.

"I have brought Lady Ninym."

There was no response. The servant opened the door regardless and ushered Ninym inside. She stepped forward, and...

"...Ah, I understand."

Her surprise lasted for only a second. Now things were coming together. Ninym smiled with comprehension.

"So, *you're* the master—"

The Signing Ceremony.

It was both a legal and a cultural function held once a decade to discuss the future of the Ulbeth Alliance. Although the subject matter varied each time slightly, the crux of the event remained the same. They would begin with individual economic situations and issues, work up to city solidarity and international affairs, and conclude with a vote on whether to maintain the Alliance or not.

Most discussion points were settled beforehand, however, leaving the preservation of the union as the central topic. Each city had the right to withdraw, but none ever did.

Of course, that was only the case of previous Signing Ceremonies. The widening cracks between the four cities grew more visible every day.

"I wonder how this Signing Ceremony will go."

"So do I. After all, the West and the South Representatives eloped just when it seemed like their cities were allies."

"There are rumors that Altie is acting strange, too."

"What can they do? Altie doesn't even have a representative. Anyway, Muldu's responsible for all these crazy weddings, right? I hear they're gathering a ton of people."

"Even if Roynock and Facrita lose their representatives, that won't be enough to take them down."

Talk of the future swirled among Ulbeth's citizens. As they waited with bated breath, the ceremony to decide their fates commenced.

This Signing Ceremony was held in Muldu's Parliament building. It was large enough to accommodate roughly one hundred people comfortably but was currently packed shoulder to shoulder with eager crowds.

When the Ulbeth Alliance was first formed, the Signing Ceremony involved only the representatives and several of their associates. However, as the event grew in significance, the representatives started competing against each other to see who could invite the most notables. The result was that each city was forced to erect a large venue.

And now, the Muldu site was jammed with dignitaries from each city.

"What a thrilling view," Wein remarked quietly. He sat in the front row of the eastern sector and looked out over the riled crowd. There were four seats on a raised platform at the innermost part of the venue, one for each representative. Agata was already in place, but the remaining three spots were still empty.

"I get why the Altie chair is vacant, but are the western and the southern cities still quarreling?"

Wein looked at each camp and found them in an uproar. Although this was entirely his fault, he'd been ignoring them since Ninym's abduction. Still, Roynock and Facrita had hardly calmed down, even without the prince's eye on them.

"I hear the groups were nearly unified, but word spread that the two strongest candidates, Rauve and Huanshe, have captured Sir Oleom and Lady Lejoutte," Kamil explained from his spot beside Wein. "Supporters of the former representatives are naturally opposed, and adversaries of the top two candidates are taking advantage of the situation as well. In all the chaos, there have been no new representatives chosen."

"The people involved are dead serious, but I'm sure it must seem absurd to those watching from the sidelines," Wein replied tiredly. "At this rate, Agata will have center stage."

"The other cities are aware of this as well. Soon enough, they'll—"

Kamil's sentence was cut off. Two men, one from Facrita and the other from Roynock, pushed through any who tried to hold them back and stepped forward.

"It seems the strongest candidates have made their way to the forefront."

"Then I suppose it's time to begin."

Wein and the others looked on as the meeting commenced.

"No need to rush," Agata remarked as the two who had shoved their way forward took their respective seats. A cold smile spread across the East Representative's face.

"Shut it, Agata. Do you have any idea how much your stunts screwed up Roynock?"

"Rauve is right. We'll be discussing your antics."

Agata couldn't hide his derision. "What an odd threat. Isn't that chaos the reason the seats that are far beyond your capabilities remain unoccupied?"

"Damn you…!"

Rauve raged with indignation, but Huanshe stepped in as if to keep him in check.

"Your words implicate you. Isn't that paramount to a confession, Sir Agata?"

"Yes, I admit it," Agata admitted passively. "However, who can criticize me? After all, I'm the only representative here."

"What…?!"

"Do you not understand? The representatives of our great Ulbeth Alliance are elected after long and careful discussion. Can someone chosen on the spot honestly be considered a true one?"

Rauve and Huanshe were humiliated. They had struggled to make it this far, yet Agata refused to acknowledge them as his equals.

"Well, so what?! The Signing Ceremony is held once a decade. Are you saying you get to run the show?!"

"That does appear to be the case." Agata did not falter, despite the intense atmosphere. "If anything, you are at fault for failing to elect proper representatives. I have done nothing wrong."

"Absurd!" Rauve howled. "Did everyone hear that?! Will you allow such tyranny?!"

Those gathered people from Roynock and Facrita shouted in protest. Even Rauve and Huanshe's critics had to agree with them on this point. Muldu's citizens naturally sided with Agata, but the clamor from the other groups made it plain they were outnumbered.

"…Sir Agata, I admit our failure to select a representative in a timely manner. However, the Signing Ceremony cannot function properly with only the East Representative. I would like you to make an exception and accept us."

"Hmph." Agata sniffed haughtily as he considered Huanshe's proposal. "An exception, you say. Yes, considering Roynock and Facrita's many years of contribution, I suppose I can allow that."

"Precisely. Our noble ancestors will be greatly pleased to know the Signing Ceremony is proceeding as intended," Huanshe agreed.

Agata snickered. "Ah, yes, our ancestors. Well, if you're going to go that far, I suppose I have no choice. I'll accept you as representatives."

Rauve clicked his tongue. "*Tsk*, you better!"

"In that case, let us begin," Huanshe proposed.

While Agata had been caught off guard, he clearly knew when something was unreasonable. The throngs of people from the southern and the western cities were relieved by his swift compliance.

However, the surprising upsets didn't end there.

"—In that case, I wish to be accepted at well."

A dignified voice rose from Agata's camp. It had come from the man standing by Wein. All present looked over as a figure advanced to the platform.

"You...? What's going on?"

"What do you mean, 'accepted'?"

Unsure what this upstart was thinking, Rauve and Huanshe eyed the man with caution and confusion while Agata stared in silence.

"I am Kamil Croon, the son of former North Representative Croon. I am here to declare myself his successor."

"So *you're* the master, Kamil," Ninym said.

Kamil smiled as she stepped into the room. "Indeed, I am. Are you surprised?"

"Truthfully, I suspected you might be pulling the strings. Only someone close to His Highness and me would realize the slaves' value as hostages. You spoke to me on my way home so you could buy time to position your men, right?"

"Yes," Kamil stated, bowing his head deeply. "I do apologize for resorting to such violent methods as abduction. However, I had to put a stop to Prince Wein. Left alone, he was going to help Agata win."

"So you're saying that Agata didn't condone this."

"That's correct. But I am not a spy for Roynock or Facrita either," Kamil clarified. "In truth, I am the son of the executed North Representative."

"...!"

Ninym couldn't hide her surprise. The look in Kamil's eyes made it apparent that he wasn't joking, and he had no reason to lie. And so her mind skipped ahead and wondered what the descendant of the North Representative could be after.

"...Do you want revenge on Ulbeth?"

"Yes," Kamil confirmed lightly. "Lady Ninym, I'm certain this nation must have proved shocking to you on multiple occasions. I'm also confident you've thought it a sinister and suffocating place, one that isn't fun at all."

"...I can't deny that."

"I was too young to understand at the time, but I heard Ulbeth was the same way while my parents were alive. They did their best to make things better—and were killed for it." Kamil sighed emptily. "I hate this place. It's nothing but hopeless people who lack innovation and celebrate the status quo. Before returning here, I'd hoped that things had improved since my parents' demise, but such a thing was foolhardy to wish for."

Ninym's frown was sympathetic. Kamil spoke of revenge, but his voice rang hollow. It sounded more like he'd accepted that there was no going back for him.

"...How exactly will you take your retribution?"

"I can't share the details. But I intend to destroy the Ulbeth Alliance."

He's serious, Ninym thought. If there was any chance of stopping him, the time was now.

"...I agree the Ulbeth Alliance hasn't left the greatest impression on me," Ninym began carefully. "Still, not everyone here is corrupt. There are plenty who weren't involved with what happened to your parents, and there are innocent children who don't know what happened. Will you punish them, too?"

"Hmph..."

After listening to Ninym, Kamil suddenly took off his jacket. The Flahm woman warily assumed a fighting stance as her opponent exposed his upper body. The deep, wide scars he bore made her want to look away.

"My pursuers gave me these parting gifts when I escaped Ulbeth." Kamil smiled. "As you say, Lady Ninym, the sins of a parent are not the sins of a child. That is logical. I will release you once everything is over. After that, return to your country and tell everyone. Tell them the foolish, illogical people of a senseless land were destroyed by their own folly—"

"...'Their own folly,'" Ninym whispered to herself as she recalled Kamil's words.

After their meeting, she was led back to the room that was her prison. She had tried to say something to Kamil, but the words refused to come when she saw the man's expression.

"I wonder how everything is going…"

Ninym had no information about the outside world, but she sensed that the Signing Ceremony was about to begin. Kamil would undoubtedly use that opportunity to reveal his relation to the North Representative. She had no idea how he would bring about Ulbeth's destruction, but there was no question that a huge commotion awaited and that her master would be caught up in it.

"Wein…"

There was no way of knowing what he was thinking or if he was even at the ceremony. The prince being who he was, he'd likely cooked up some incomprehensible scheme. Nonetheless, Ninym cared for his safety above all else. She prayed even though she knew no smiling god would hear her.

"That's ridiculous…Croon's son…?!" Rauve exclaimed, his eyes large.

"But the whole family was wiped out…!" Huanshe chimed in, unable to mask his worry.

"I have proof. Here is a Croon family heirloom and a document signed by my parents confirming my bloodline. They were given to me when I escaped Ulbeth. Only one family per city may become its representative. As a legitimate descendent, I meet every qualification."

Kamil produced an exquisite black short sword engraved with

the emblem of Altie. Such a fine article wasn't easy to come by. However—

"You think that proves anything?!"

"Rauve is right. If this is all you have…"

Accepting Kamil as the North Representative would be a considerable nuisance. Thus, all other representatives had to reject him, or so one might think.

"No, I recognize his claim as legitimate." Unlike the other two, Agata advocated for Kamil. "He is indeed Croon's child."

"Agata! Do you realize what you're saying?!"

"If there's a North Representative, you'll be at a disadvantage, too…!"

"'Disadvantage'?" Agata repeated, flatly rejecting the stubborn arguments. "It's more unusual to leave the seat unoccupied. With his participation, the Signing Ceremony can function as intended. Our ancestors will be quite pleased."

It was sound logic, and the audience went silent. Rauve, however, only grew more infuriated.

"You've been plotting this all along, haven't you?! I'll never accept this!"

"Indeed. I cannot readily welcome such abnormal circumstances."

"Didn't you want me to make an exception for yourselves?"

"This is totally different!" Rauve bellowed, dismissing Agata's sarcasm. "Kamil! You don't belong here! Agata might condone this, but we sure as hell don't! If you understand, then leave now!"

Kamil took a step forward. "No, you will be the ones to leave. I have no intention of recognizing you as representatives either."

"What…?!"

"There are others more suited to the position, after all."

A stir ran through the crowd. Everyone knew whom Kamil was referring to.

"Hey, calm down! This brat doesn't know what he's talkin' about—" Rauve surveyed the crowd as he shouted. Then he spotted something, and his eyes shot open.

The reaction drew Haunshe's attention. He looked to where Rauve was staring and realized Kamil's words hadn't been the only source of commotion.

"It—it can't be…"

Two figures among the quiet Altie group of attendees removed their hoods. There was no mistaking their identities.

"Oleom…and Lejoutte…?!"

The East and the West Representatives, who had officially eloped, were standing right there.

"Listen well!" Oleom addressed the confused crowd in a strong and gallant voice. "Representative Lejoutte and I did not elope! Two people spread baseless rumors, tarnished our dignity, and held us against our will… Rauve and Huanshe!"

"We've already subdued the other candidates. You won't talk your way out of this," Lejoutte added.

Rauve and Huanshe trembled. As Oleom and Lejoutte claimed, they had conspired to seize power by spreading rumors of an elopement while the representatives were dealing with the marriage campaign.

"A certain person wondered if, instead of running away together, Oleom and Lejoutte were being held captive somewhere," Kamil stated. "I sent my own search party and discovered that hunch was correct. You should have killed them when you had the chance."

"Ngh…!"

Rauve and Huanshe gritted their teeth. The crowd now viewed them not as suspects but as criminals.

"...Guards, what are you waiting for?" Agata asked after keeping silent thus far. "They are culprits who tried to steal honorable positions through unjust means. Take them away."

"W-wait, Agata! This is a mistake!"

"Hey, quit it! Get offa me!"

Rauve and Huanshe resisted arrest, but several guards quickly removed them from the building. No one tried to stop them. A hush fell on the assembly after the pair left kicking and screaming.

"—Well then."

As if to break the heavy silence, Oleom and Lejoutte stepped on the platform with noticeably loud footsteps.

"We will resume our positions from this point forward. Seeing as the one who aided us was none other than Sir Kamil, we shall accept him as the North Representative," Oleom announced.

"If there are any objections, speak now," Lejoutte declared.

None said a word.

Agata had already accepted Kamil, and he now had the approval of the two other proper representatives. There was no room for objection.

"In that case, Sir Kamil shall be instated as the North Representative," Oleom said.

Clapping and cheers erupted from the Altie camp, who had been containing themselves. The other groups offered a smattering of applause, too.

Showered by accolades, Agata's young aide stood on the platform as the new North Representative.

"I wish to thank the three of you for allowing me this position."

Kamil bowed deeply. "Next, please forgive my brevity, but I'd like to make a declaration as the North Representative. We, the northern city of Altie, are withdrawing from the Ulbeth Alliance."

Altie was withdrawing from the Ulbeth Alliance.

Unrest rippled through the throngs when they heard Kamil's announcement.

"Is he serious?! Withdrawal?!"

"What are you talking about, North Representative?!"

"What will happen to us?!"

The people grew louder. To them, the Ulbeth Alliance had always been a nation of four city-states and the bedrock of their value system. They'd never allow someone to destroy that foundation. Citizens from Altie were the only ones to applaud.

Kamil pressed on despite the audience's confusion.

"Sir Oleom and Lady Lejoutte have already consented."

No one had expected this. They couldn't imagine their own leaders approving of such a reckless proposal.

"Is that true, Sir Oleom?!"

"Lady Lejoutte! Why would you do such a thing?!"

Criticism arose from the crowd, but the two maintained their silence. Their silence was taken as consent, and the confusion rapidly turned to rage.

"It would be insane to withdraw!"

"That's right! You must reconsider!"

The four representatives sat and watched as furious voices sounded from every direction in the hall.

"Does the north plan to betray us?!"

Kamil's face twisted at this question, and as he answered, his voice rose to a roar. "You dare speak of betrayal. 'Betrayal' implies an equal relationship! Being cut down by those who one-sidedly exploited and subjugated you is not 'betrayal'! That is 'abandonment'!"

Once again, the audience went quiet. Altie's ostracization and victimization were indisputable.

"B-but, North Representative. You'll be on your own if you leave the Alliance. There will be nothing stopping us from overtaking you."

Kamil's expression soured further as he listened.

"How pathetic. Rather than reflect on your own actions, you grow defensive and hurl threats. Do you still not understand that attitude is the very reason you've been abandoned? You should worry about yourselves first." Kamil mercilessly dismissed their complaints and continued to drive his point home. "Or are you claiming we have no right to withdraw? In that case, state so plainly! Say the Signing Ceremony and our value system are nothing but a sham! Our Ulbeth customs you killed my parents to protect! Our traditions! Our framework! It's all a convenient illusion! Come on, out with it!"

The hatred was thick in Kamil's voice. Yet at the same time, several people surely noticed the tinge of hope behind it. Despite rallying against the Ulbeth Alliance, he still hoped. He wanted someone to stop him, even if it meant he'd be killed. Kamil prayed that someone would decry the Signing Ceremony, the symbol of the Ulbeth.

If that happened…

Ulbeth's authority would be tarnished, and people might realize the nation was not invincible. It could spark change and bring them a step closer to the fresh possibilities his parents had longed for.

However…

"…"

No one moved. The people only looked at each other and exchanged fervent whispers.

"…*Pft.*"

Kamil wasn't even disappointed. He already knew what needed to be done. He would conclude the Signing Ceremony without incident and sign the secession papers. The young man's heart felt dry and cold, but he turned to the task at hand.

"May I say something?" Agata spoke up out of nowhere.

"…Sir Agata, don't tell me you've changed your mind?"

Kamil glared at the East Representative. The emotion in his eyes differed from his hatred of Ulbeth.

"No, that's not it. Even if I were opposed, I wouldn't say so."

"Well then, what is it?" Kamil pressed.

Agata took a breath.

"As of this moment, I resign as Muldu's East Representative."

His statement was simple, but it took Kamil and the audience several moments to process.

"…W-wait! What are you talking about?!" Once he'd processed the unexpected turn of events, Kamil asked a panicked question, but Agata remained unbothered.

"Moreover, I wish to recommend a successor."

One figure rose from the eastern camp. Everyone present stared in shock when they realized who it was.

"Wein Salema Arbalest. He shall be the next East Representative," Agata announced.

The prince of Natra smiled.

A bolt from the blue.

No other words could describe the scene.

Wein made his way through the crowd and leisurely stepped onto the platform. Many were still in denial, but there could be no refuting that Agata had called the prince's name.

"Y-you must be joking!" Kamil exclaimed, speaking for the crowd. "Why is Prince Wein here?! Him, a representative? That's ridiculous... Besides, he doesn't even have the qualifications!"

Representatives could come only from specific families. Agata fulfilled this condition, but Wein obviously wasn't a relative.

"He is my *adopted* son."

The audience was dumbstruck once again.

Childless couples often took in orphaned children, and the nobility openly accepted the kids of other aristocrats to preserve their own family lines.

Be that as it may...

"H-have you gone mad?! Adopting a foreign prince?! That's not even possi—"

"It is. After all, we have no system that forbids it," Agata insisted.

Kamil was unable to reply.

It was a reasonable reaction. No one could have ever guessed at such a turn of events. It was the first of its kind in Ulbeth's history. As no one had considered such a thing before, there was no legislation forbidding it.

"N-Natra will never permit such an outrage."

"Ha-ha-ha. You're so funny, Sir Kamil," Wein said on the platform. "I'm a prince. I make the rules."

Everyone thought the whole thing was absurd, but they were powerless to argue. Wein *was* a royal, and it was common knowledge he essentially ran Natra.

"Ngh… But…!" Kamil looked at the other two representatives. "Sir Oleom! Lady Lejoutte! Are you fine with this?!"

When Kamil had saved them, they'd promised to recognize him as the North Representative and approve of his withdrawal from the Alliance. Wein, on the other hand, had ruined both of their lives. Surely, they'd do anything to stop him from becoming an official of their nation.

"I accept him as East Representative."

"I accept Prince Wein as well."

Kamil shot up from his chair. "What—why?! How could you agree?!"

What were they thinking? Why would they allow this despite the obvious disadvantages?

Oleom shook his head heavily. "It's just a matter of sequence, Sir Kamil."

"Honestly… To think everything would turn out like he said," appended Lejoutte.

"'A matter of sequence'…?" Kamil feverishly ruminated over these words. Then, it struck him. "No, it can't be. You must be joking!"

The newly appointed North Representative turned to face Wein. "You found them first…?!"

"What strange fate for the three of us to reunite like this."

Shortly before the Signing Ceremony, Wein met with Oleom and Lejoutte in a certain mansion.

"…How did you know where we were being held?"

Rauve and Huanshe had trapped the two in a house, but they were abruptly rescued by mysterious men and brought to Muldu.

"You can thank Agata. He has a private army even his closest aide doesn't know about, plus a detailed map of each city's hidden alleys and niches. Goodness, he's still sharp as a tack," Wein explained with an air of admiration.

"So what will you do with us?" Lejoutte questioned.

"I want you to recognize me as the next East Representative at the Signing Ceremony."

"Huh?"

Lejoutte blinked, and Oleom answered with confusion.

"…I have no idea what your intentions are, but it's pointless. You don't have the qualifications to become a representative."

"Oh, don't worry about that. I'll figure something out. You just have to accept me once I meet those conditions."

Oleom and Lejoutte looked at each other for a moment and nodded.

"…All right. Whatever will get us out of here."

"Oh, one more thing."

"What?!" Lejoutte stared at him. "Aren't you being a bit greedy?"

"I saved both of you, so one request for each."

"…All right, what is it?"

"Let Kamil think he saved you."

Oleom's and Lejoutte's furrowed brows suggested they didn't understand, but Wein soon clarified.

"Kamil launched his own search team. I'll provide a safe hideout, so pretend to be locked up there. After that, I'll point him in your direction so he can locate you. Kamil will probably ask for a reward like my first request. Keep our meeting a secret and do what he says."

"I—I really don't get it…" Lejoutte admitted hopelessly.

Oleom's expression indicated he was struggling to comprehend as well.

"So…you want us to trick Kamil? But why in such a roundabout manner?"

"That's easy," Wein said with a smile. "Because he laid a hand on my Heart."

"Well, there's not much to think about. I'm Natra's prince, and I joined the family of East Representative. That's it," Wein stated breezily.

It was a massive understatement, but Kamil's mind was occupied by another matter.

I had no idea Wein met Oleom and Lejoutte! Or that Agata chose a new East Representative! I thought they only knew I'd become North Representative!

Oleom and Lejoutte had kept this information from him. Their intention, of course, was to impede his plans. If Kamil wanted to destroy the Alliance, he would have to stop Wein at any cost.

"…Citizens of Muldu! Will you stand for this?!" With no other recourse, Kamil tried to provoke the bewildered populace of the eastern city. "Although he has Sir Agata's approval, he is still a foreign prince! Do you honestly think you will benefit?!"

A predecessor's endorsement improved a representative candidate's chances, but there was no guarantee since political dealings within a faction often determined a successor. Furthermore, while Agata had no children of his own, he possessed many relatives.

Muldu had been on the decline until recently, but most people still coveted the position. If Kamil could stir them to action—

"Hey, everyone," Wein addressed the crowd. "Shut up and watch. I'll lead you to victory."

A chill ran through Kamil.

This is Wein Salema Arbalest...!

He had thought he understood the prince's might. Despite Wein's cheery and easygoing demeanor, his alarmingly devious schemes had shocked Kamil more than once.

But that was only the tip of the iceberg. Kamil felt Wein's overwhelming political presence in his very bones as the two squared off.

"I'd like your cooperation, Kamil."

Wein looked over at the other man and grinned. The Muldu camp had fallen obediently silent. No, it wasn't just them; everyone was waiting with bated breath. All it had taken was a few words.

"Very impressive."

"It's just business as usual to me."

After this brief exchange, Agata stood and Wein took his place. None objected to the birth of the new East Representative.

"Well, then. Sorry for cutting to the chase, but let's pick up where we left off. Altie wants to withdraw from the Alliance, right?" Wein asked. "Allow me to make a suggestion. I believe Ulbeth should remain, northern city and all."

Kamil grimaced. However, this wasn't because Wein disagreed with his opinion.

I thought that Muldu wanted to unite *the Alliance...?*

If that was Agata's goal, as an ally, it should have been Wein's as well. Perhaps he'd felt unprepared to handle the situation and had elected to maintain things instead.

©Falmaro

It's useless. I have no clue what he's thinking.

Both Agata and Wein had far more education and experience as statesmen than Kamil. He couldn't hope to understand the inner workings of their minds.

There's no point overthinking it. Just press forward!

Kamil spoke with resolve. "As I've said before, Ulbeth exploited Altie. Remaining in this system will do us no good!"

"That was true up until now, right? With you as their representative, I'm sure the northern city won't suffer the same abuse."

Wein had a point, and Kamil mentally clicked his tongue. Yes, emotional turmoil aside, he could easily lead Altie and revitalize it while remaining in the Alliance.

"Also, since you so elegantly dodged the subject earlier, what are your plans after independence? Altie depends on the rest of Ulbeth for farming, foreign diplomacy, and trade. You'd have a hard enough time scratching out a living even without the possibility of invaders. And we can't discount the notion that the other three cities and just about everyone else nearby will be looking for their chances to strike. I find this hard to believe, but maybe…you just want to secede and couldn't care less if you're destroyed?"

He was right. Kamil *didn't* care. It was his greatest wish to see the Ulbeth Alliance swallowed by some foreign power after Altie withdrew.

Of course, not many knew this. Kamil needed another explanation for most of the northerners in the crowd. And that was—

"You've been negotiating with the Casskard Kingdom to the north, right?"

"…"

Kamil scowled as Wein hit the nail on the head.

He would sell the untethered city of Altie to Casskard to ensure its protection. Casskard would then serve as a bridgehead against the other three cities. It had been a plausible strategy…until last year anyway.

Wein pressed on.

"The West is in the midst of a major food shortage, and Casskard is no exception. It'd be one thing if they were prosperous like Facrita, but Casskard has already said that they don't want to upset the other three cities by taking the northern one, right?"

H-how does he…?!

Wein couldn't have known. It was impossible. Yet he spoke as if he'd seen everything himself and shone a light on the truth.

"*Tsk-tsk*, Kamil. You shouldn't conceal such important details from your friends."

This man…!

Kamil clenched his teeth and looked over at the assembled Altie people. Sure enough, worry was spreading. He couldn't afford to lose support here.

"Spare me your reckless lies!" Kamil shouted, hoping to cut this topic short. "I agree that Altie would flourish in the Alliance if I were representative. However, we cannot simply clear away the disgrace thrust upon us! Or are you shamelessly suggesting we overlook the past and form an equal relationship?!"

By this point, Kamil's only option was an emotional appeal. Even Wein couldn't overturn the northern city's dislike of the rest of Ulbeth. He would needle at those feelings to gain secession.

And yet…

"Well, I thought you might say that," Wein replied with a light nod. "So let me offer some reparations."

The prince of Natra presented a document.

"Wh-what's this?"

"The answer key to the Ulbeth Alliance. I wrote it myself."

Every representative immediately understood what he meant. Kamil's hands shook as he received the document.

"It'll unravel the Alliance's tangled relationships. If you have it… Well, need I explain further?"

Kamil had watched Wein ruin Roynock and Facrita's authority firsthand. If the prince spoke the truth, he could re-create that success.

"I'm giving this to you," Wein said. "With it, you'll have a huge advantage over the others. Think about it. Nothing would feel better than controlling those thorns in your side, right? However, the information is only good if the four cities stay together. If even one leaves the union, the significant shift in relationships will reduce that sheet to a worthless scrap of paper."

"…!"

Something cold like fear gripped Kamil.

I gave the Alliance-hating north a new alternative, but Prince Wein is trying to dissuade them! Rather than forget our hatred, he wants us to stay and clear it…!

It was an unusual concept. How had Wein used the prospect of strength to captivate Altie instead of giving them the hope for escape?

Altie's citizens were inspired. Reigning as victors in a familiar situation was more captivating than an unknown future of independence.

"…Sir Kamil, I also wish for the Alliance to continue," Oleom stated, breaking his silence. "I agree that we were foolish. Ulbeth should have been more honest with Altie—no, with one another as a whole. The past cannot be erased, but we should take this as a lesson and move forward."

"Keep your pretty, meaningless words…! Aren't you worried Altie will stay only to seek revenge?!"

"Yes. I'm nervous, but overcoming those challenges will make Ulbeth even stronger."

"It will probably sink without overcoming anything!"

"That is why we're here. To ensure that it doesn't."

Both Oleom and Lejoutte remained in staunch favor of the Alliance, and the same sentiment was spreading through the audience. Kamil had to say something to stop them, but he could manage only to express frustration and resentment.

"…Why, Prince Wein? Why are you getting in my way?!"

"Because you touched my Heart," Wein replied. "Well, that's half the reason anyway. I also saw something pretty good."

"What…?"

Several days earlier, Wein was bidding good-bye to the rescued Oleom and Lejoutte.

"You know, I was wondering, what will you do when everything is over?" the prince asked.

"What will we do?"

The pair of representatives tilted their heads.

"I figured you'd be mad your factions betrayed you after all that hard work."

"Wasn't that your fault?" Oleom pointed out.

"Well, yeah," Wein admitted casually. "It's not much, but I can help you escape if you want."

Oleom and Lejoutte considered the idea for a moment before bursting into laughter.

"The thought is enough. We've both decided to stay in Ulbeth," Lejoutte stated.

"Why? With your skills, you'd be fine in any other country."

"Prince Wein, do you know about North Representative Croon

and his wife? The ones who were executed twenty years ago?" asked Lejoutte. Wein nodded, and so she continued. "They hoped to change Ulbeth for the better and never tried to run despite many opportunities."

"The Alliance is twisted; the rejection of the North Representative is the worst example of this. However, we'd never live up to the Croons' legacy if we fled."

"We will correct Ulbeth our way. That's what we've decided after learning how they lived."

Oleom's and Lejoutte's eyes sparkled with strength.

"Kamil, you abandoned the Alliance a long time ago…but it has more potential than you think," Wein mused with a smile.

During the Signing Ceremony, the two supposedly eloped representatives returned, and new North and East Representatives were chosen. The day saw many ups and downs, but the Ulbeth Alliance was still whole at the end.

In a room of Agata's mansion…

"Nrghh…"

Ninym was splayed across the bed.

"Cheer up. It wasn't your fault," Wein assured her with a smile. He sat down beside her. Consoling the young woman was proving difficult this time.

"I didn't help at all. In fact, I got in your way…"

Kamil had kidnapped Ninym, but Wein's rescue team found her before she could break out. They escaped after most of Kamil's staff had left for the Signing Ceremony. Wein had been hugely relieved to see Ninym safe.

"I want to disappear… I want to become a shell…"

She wasn't feeling all too glad about it, though.

Everything worked out, thanks to Wein, but…

Ninym's weakness would likely trip her up in the future. She'd probably end up involving Wein as well, and realizing as much made her squirm irritably on the mattress. She was ordinarily quick to recover and return to business as usual, but her heart felt too defeated.

After Ninym was done twisting and turning, she tried to burrow under the sheets like a small, underground animal.

"Hey, Ninym."

©Falmaro

"Eek!"

Wein suddenly picked the girl up, sheets and all, and sat her on his lap.

"It's my fault you were kidnapped, too. We both made mistakes. Let's just reflect and be glad we're safe."

"Mm…" Ninym blushed pink and gave a tiny nod.

Wein stroked her pale hair. "Besides, I messed up way more than you. You're adorably clumsy by comparison."

"…Now that you mention it, yeah."

"Wait, you agree?"

"By the way, Wein, I heard something about you becoming Agata's adopted son?"

"This was supposed to be the part where you'd cheer me up."

Wein quickly put Ninym down and tried to bolt for the door, but she snared him with the sheets.

"What were you thinking?! King Owen, your *actual* father, is still alive!"

"Uh, well, it was my only way out."

"Need I remind you this will be a huge problem when we get home…?!"

"Yeah, that's why I'd be really appreciative if you helped me cook up an explanation."

Ninym stretched out Wein's cheeks as far as they'd go. "*Hahhh.* Honestly… Everyone's going to side with Princess Falanya if you keep toying with foreign countries like this," Ninym half joked, exhausted.

"Sounds perfect. It's about time Natra's citizens wake up from their dream."

The prince slipped out of the sheets.

"Wein…?"

©Falmaro

"I'm going to talk with Agata for a bit. Make sure everything is ready to head home. Oh, and remind any slaves who want to come along."

With that, Wein took his leave.

Ninym pressed the sheets to her chest. They still had his warmth.

"...Diona Croon, the wife of former North Representative Gerde Croon, was my daughter."

Wein sat in the reception room of Agata's mansion as its master gave an address.

"She was a lively child and my hope for the future. As Diona grew older, she sensed Ulbeth's oppressive air and began searching for a way to break the deadlock."

"And that's how she met Gerde?"

"Yes. He mourned Ulbeth's future as well. It was inevitable the two fell for each other."

Agata's gaze seemed to be staring at a scene far, far away. At happier days long lost.

"One was a direct descendant of the North Representative, the other of the East. They couldn't associate without repercussions. Yet to create a brighter future for Ulbeth, they joined forces, married, and had a child. This became a source of confidence for them, and they felt it was their duty to create a wonderful world for their baby."

"But—they failed."

Agata gave a heavy nod. As someone who was neither there at the time nor a citizen of Ulbeth, Wein didn't know the details of the couple's downfall, but he understood it wasn't something spoken of lightly.

"I sought desperately to save them from execution. However, when I spoke with my daughter from her jail cell, she told me not to bother."

"Why?"

"Diona was concerned that Muldu and Altie would destroy each other and knew I'd be suspected of collusion if I defended her. If both cities fell, foreign nations would be quick to step in."

"She made a choice like that, knowing it would mean her death..." Wein shook his head.

Agata wore an empty smile as he said, "My daughter cared for Ulbeth more than her own life. Even so, she worried about her child. Diona asked me to save him, so I secretly took him out of Ulbeth."

"To Casskard?"

Agata nodded. "Diona was executed as a traitor. As her father, people were suspicious of me, and my political opponents were always looking for an opening. My hands were tied, and I could never check on the child in Casskard."

"You're saying he just showed up here one day?"

"That's right. It was about ten years ago. He had a different name, but I immediately knew he shared my daughter's blood... And that he hated both the Ulbeth Alliance and me."

A heavy quiet settled over Agata and Wein. The prince waited patiently for the older man to regain his composure.

"Honestly, I'm sick of Ulbeth, too."

"That's reasonable. It killed your daughter."

"Regardless, Diona entrusted me with a duty. She said she wanted to leave Ulbeth in my hands despite her own lack of success. Those words drove me onward as I continued to serve as East

Representative. But no matter what I accomplish, my daughter is still dead, and Ulbeth hasn't changed. I've failed just as she did.

"That's why I didn't care if my grandson, if Kamil, destroyed Ulbeth. In fact, death by his hand was the best end I could ask for. I decided to help him secretly."

"...I see," Wein replied. "It's all coming together. Kamil aimed to annihilate the Ulbeth Alliance, and you aided him from behind the scenes. However, the famine in the West messed it all up."

Agata's mouth twisted wryly. "Indeed. The idea was to provoke Altie into an armed uprising, take control of the Signing Ceremony, and swiftly finish off Ulbeth with an invasion from Casskard. However, your stunt at the Gathering of the Chosen cost me that chance."

"Sorry," Wein replied, not the least bit repentant. "So...you invited me here to team up with Kamil?"

"I've seen your resourcefulness. Casskard fell short, so Kamil needed another tactic. That's why I invited you under the pretext of helping unite the Alliance."

"No wonder you wanted me to stick around. You were buying enough time for Kamil to make the first move."

"However, that tactic also failed... Because you raised Muldu's influence with astonishing skill and speed."

Agata must have been on pins and needles. He had initially planned for Wein to team up with his grandson, but the prince's efforts had produced incredible results.

"Your success flustered Kamil, and he soon considered you an enemy... I'll never forgive myself for choosing such a terrible candidate."

"You shouldn't have invited a troublemaker."

"Ah, so you admit it, then?"

"It's something I've come to realize only recently."

Wein and Agata exchanged brief grins.

"…I do have one question. When did you first become suspicious of Kamil?"

"Around the time we bought up the slaves and weapons to mess with Roynock and Facrita," Wein answered. "I shouldn't have been able to purchase that many. Arms are made for battle, so no one keeps a ready supply unless they're fighting with a neighbor. Yet somehow, the northern city had plenty. In other words, someone connected to Altie believed that war would break out soon."

"I see…"

"Plus, Kamil was able to purchase all those weapons for me even though battle was supposedly on the horizon. I figured Altie had decided the threat was gone and didn't need the surplus, or Kamil had convinced the city to sell them. It was suspicious all around. You can never be too careful."

"I see… I already knew this, but we truly stood no chance."

Agata smiled weakly. Wein couldn't have staged the scuffle at the Gathering of the Chosen otherwise, but the Holy Elite was no less impressed. This young prince was a remarkable character.

"I have a question, too. Did you know from the start that Kamil abducted Ninym?"

"I did recognize that he was acting strange. That was why I expressed my surprise. I was almost certain it was Kamil."

"Is that what you meant?"

"Indeed." Agata nodded with a quiet sigh. "And now here we are."

"Thanks. I get it now."

"Well then, I believe I have one small, final request."

Agata rose and bowed his head to Wein.

"Please, forgive Kamil…!" the older man entreated desperately. "I'm an inferior substitute, but burn and boil me if you wish. To Kamil, I am the despicable person who abandoned his parents. However, to me, Kamil is a reminder of my daughter's legacy. I beg of you…!"

Kamil had sparked Wein's imperial wrath by daring to lay a hand on Ninym. There was no future for him unless Agata appeased the dragon. No matter where Kamil tried to hide, he would be burned to a crisp as soon as Wein returned to Natra. Agata believed it was his final duty to prevent this fate.

Wein wore a cheeky, sunny expression. "Forgiveness, huh? And you're even begging… I suppose I've tortured him enough, and Oleom gave me the business deal I wanted. I'm not mad anymore."

"…Really?"

"Ninym said she was treated well, and your input helped us rescue her during the Signing Ceremony. She'll get annoyed if I lash out at anyone else."

Wein clearly wasn't lying. Agata let out an instinctive sigh of relief.

"—But I'll kill you next time and turn Ulbeth to ash. Don't forget that."

That was no fib either. The East Representative felt a chill course down his spine.

"Oh, I'll also leave you in charge of Muldu, Agata."

"That's fine…but are you sure?"

"Yeah, I can't manage territory way out here anyway."

Wein's homeland of Natra was in the far north, whereas Ulbeth resided on the coast. Unless someone had a transportation spell, it was impossible to govern both.

"Besides, while I imagine you don't want to hear this from me, the Ulbeth Alliance has a rough road ahead. Altie won't be happy if Kamil doesn't make the most of his answer key, but the other three cities will grow resentful if he uses it *too* well. And make sure to remember that sheet will only be good for about one year."

"…I suppose that makes sense."

Wein's answer key was based on current information. Circumstances would change as developments arose, and even Wein couldn't predict everything. It was incredible enough that he'd plotted things out for an entire year.

"We'll put any corrections or additions you may have to good use."

"Take care not to be restricted by obligations like tradition either. Stuff like that shouldn't mean ignoring a decision you know is right. Such things are no problem for me, but I'm not so sure about Kamil."

At the end of the day, Kamil was a man with a strong sense of responsibility. He wouldn't abandon his duty as a representative, even if he hadn't planned on actually staying in the role. Wein wasn't certain if that moral nature was for better or worse, however.

"Do your best to support your grandson in my place."

"Thank you, Prince Wein." Agata gave a deep, deep bow. "Kamil, Oleom, and Lejoutte… I will spend what little time I have left in this world helping Ulbeth's young leaders transform our country."

Wein smiled. "I hope I can enjoy a hearty welcome the next time I visit, Foster Father."

Agata smiled in return and nodded. "Yes. Look forward to it, my son."

* * *

And so the chaos in the Ulbeth Alliance was temporarily quelled. It was not a major disturbance in the grand scheme of the continent's history. However, future historians eventually realized the immense impact Wein Salema Arbalest's actions had on world events. This tumultuous era became known as the "Great War of Kings."

The climax slowly inched ever closer—

Afterword

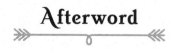

It's been a while, everyone. This is Toru Toba.

Thank you very much for picking up the ninth volume of *Genius Prince*. The theme this time is "The Binding Thread of Fate!" Whether we like it or not, our lives are connected to various destinies. They can be both a blessing and a curse. I hope you enjoyed discovering how Wein runs wild in a nation trapped by its own fate.

I also have exciting news. *Genius Prince* managed to get an anime! It's hard to believe since there's no magic and the new characters are almost always men! But it's real! Yay!

When my head editor invited me out to celebrate, they brought a lovely cake with the words *Congrats! How About Treason?* written on it. It was too surreal. (And delicious.)

And now for my usual thanks and apologies.

First, to my editor, Ohara. This was the tightest of tight deadlines. I'm so sorry… I don't think I've ever given you so much trouble. Please forgive me!

I caused my illustrator, Falmaro, a lot of trouble as well. I didn't mean to send the manuscript late and give you a crazy schedule. Still, the color insert of Ninym is like a stunning SSR trading card. You have my sincerest gratitude…!

I also can't thank you, the readers, enough. There's no question your support is why *Genius Prince* hit such a huge milestone. I'm greatly looking forward to the day we can enjoy watching the anime together.

Emuda's manga adaptation has also been a huge hit on the *Manga Up!* app, so please be sure to check it out!